Have It
Easy
Even in
Another
World!

7

Please...come back soon... I need you...

She wanted to be nearer to Jade, even if only a little, so she braced herself against the wall and ascended the stairs of a watchtower with a clear view of the Amagi Pass.

CONTENTS

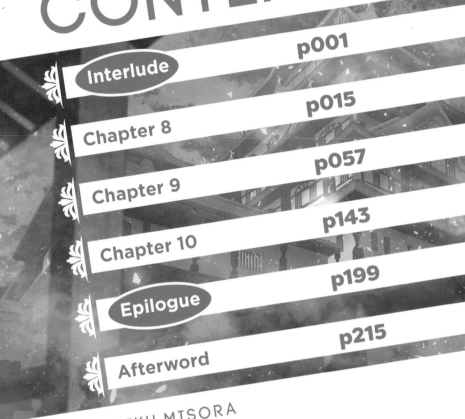

RIKU MISORA
ILLUSTRATION BY
SACRANECO

High School Prodigies
Have It Easy Even in
Another World!

High School Prodigies Have It Easy Even in Another World!

7

Riku Misora

Illustration by SACRANECO

YEN ON

NEW YORK

High School Prodigies Have It Easy Even in Another World! 7

Riku Misora

TRANSLATION BY NATHANIEL HIROSHI THRASHER
COVER ART BY SACRANECO

CHOUJIN KOUKOUSEI TACHI HA ISEKAI DEMO YOYU DE IKINUKU YOUDESU! Vol. 7
Copyright © 2018 Riku Misora
Illustrations copyright © 2018 Sacraneco
First published in Japan in 2018 by SB Creative, Tokyo.
English translation rights arranged with SB Creative, Tokyo through Tuttle-Mori Agency, Inc., Tokyo.

English translation © 2022 by Yen Press, LLC

Yen On
150 West 30th Street, 19th Floor
New York, NY 10001

Visit us at yenpress.com
facebook.com/yenpress ★ twitter.com/yenpress
yenpress.tumblr.com ★ instagram.com/yenpress

First Yen On Edition: December 2022
Edited by Yen On Editorial: Jordan Blanco
Designed by Yen Press Design: Liz Parlett

Yen On is an imprint of Yen Press, LLC.
The Yen On name and logo are trademarks of Yen Press, LLC.

Library of Congress Cataloging-in-Publication Data
Names: Misora, Riku, author. | Sacraneco, illustrator. | Thrasher, Nathaniel Hiroshi, translator.
Title: High school prodigies have it easy even in another world! / Riku Misora ; illustration by Sacraneco ; translation by Nathaniel Hiroshi Thrasher.
Other titles: Chōjin-Kokoseitachi wa Isekai demo Yoyu de Ikinuku Yōdesu! English
Identifiers: LCCN 2020016894 | ISBN 9781975309725 (v. 1 ; trade paperback) |
ISBN 9781975309749 (v. 2 ; trade paperback) | ISBN 9781975309763 (v.3 ; trade paperback) |
ISBN 9781975309787 (v. 4 ; trade paperback) | ISBN 9781975309800 (v. 5 ; trade paperback) |
ISBN 9781975309824 (v. 6 ; trade paperback) | ISBN 9781975350086 (v. 7 ; trade paperback)
Subjects: CYAC: Fantasy. | Gifted persons—Fiction. | Imaginary places—Fiction | Magic—Fiction.
Classification: LCC PZ7.M6843377 Hi 2020 | DDC [Fic]—dc23
LC record available at https://lccn.loc.gov/2020016894

ISBNs: 978-1-9753-5008-6 (paperback)
978-1-9753-5009-3 (ebook)

10 9 8 7 6 5 4 3 2 1

LSC-C

Printed in the United States of America

❧ The Nobles' Fates ❧

One day, a great shift took place in the Freyjagard Empire.

The Bluebloods had long been at odds with the Four Grand-masters. Unwilling to suffer any longer, they staged an armed upris-ing. Working together, the Blueblood aristocrats raised an army that spanned the entire empire. They targeted any organizations and aristocrats who supported the Four Grandmasters. The Blue-bloods denounced their enemies as unfaithful to Freyjagard's founder, Emperor Gottfried, and all who were disloyal were crushed by mili-tary might, allowing the Bluebloods to seize control of the nation in all the ways that mattered. Thanks to their swift blitzkrieg tactics and a plan they'd spent ages refining, the Lindworm administration's sup-porters had no time to coordinate a response.

And the Blueblood efforts were hardly confined to the country-side. The effects were felt even in Drachen, the Emperor domain's capital.

Leading this rebellion was Archduke Lucius von Weltenbruger, commander of the Bluebloods and nephew of the emperor that Lind-worm deposed. Weltenbruger's backroom dealings placed his support-ers among the capital's guard, rendering the force useless against his coup. After securing a route to the grandmaster's estate, Weltenbruger ordered what precious few mages he had to deploy an anti-magic barrier around the building, leaving it helpless against his troops.

His aim was to execute the one grandmaster who had stayed behind to govern the empire in lieu of joining the New World campaign—Neuro ul Levias.

The soldiers protecting the grandmaster's estate expected the imperial nobles to be on their side, and the sudden betrayal left them unequipped to defend. They crumpled like wet paper before the surprise attack. Weltenbruger made it all the way to Neuro's office with ease and had his men hold the grandmaster at swordpoint.

However, that was as far as he got. Everything had been going swimmingly up until then, but that was where it all went wrong.

The moment they leveled their weapons at Neuro, all the Bluebloods' ambitions were dashed.

And why, you might ask?

Because there was a young man who'd anticipated their plan as though he'd been a part of it—Masato Sanada, prodigy businessman.

On Earth, none could match Masato's business acumen. The people went so far as to dub him the "Devil of Finance." For him, predicting the future by tracking the flow of goods was child's play. Once he deduced how much of a commodity was being purchased, and where the transactions took place, Masato could determine the precise landscape of the world, present and future.

That was why, ever since his days spent handling logistics in Elm, he'd known everything. Not only had he been aware that the empire was on the verge of a massive civil war, he'd also anticipated who would start it.

Armed with that knowledge, he turned to Lakan after breaking ties with Elm. With Shenmei's assistance, he formed a contract with a Lakan mercenary group and took them right to Neuro.

Masato needed to protect Neuro during the coming upheaval.

Neuro heeded Masato's warning and had the mercenaries stand alert in the grandmaster's estate. In short, Neuro enlisted them as his personal army. And because he did so outside of the empire's systems and frameworks, the Bluebloods were ignorant of that alliance.

That oversight was the Bluebloods' undoing.

The moment their strike team was certain they had Neuro cornered, the Lakan mercenaries took them by surprise and mowed them down.

Losing Weltenbruger during an already messy and chaotic war caused the entire Bluebloods insurrection to fall apart from the grandmaster's estate outward.

"We've finished the sweep, Chancellor Advisor. The area is secure."

It was evening, and the twilit sky over the grandmaster's estate in Drachen cast the estate's entrance in bright crimson.

After receiving the mercenary captain's report, Masato thanked the captain for how he and his men had met his expectations to a tee. "Good. Nice goin'. I gotta hand it to you, you Qinglong Gang guys work quick."

The viridian-clad mercenaries thrust out their chests with pride. Confident grins spread across their tanned faces.

"Of course. We Lakan sellswords have a motto: Be good, be fast, be reliable."

"Loyalty ain't worth a single stinking ira. We're more motivated than those imperial grunts'll ever be."

"We sure as hell don't come cheap, but we make damn sure we earn our keep."

"That's what I like to hear," Masato replied. "A man who respects the value of money is a man I can trust. Glad to be doin' business with you guys."

"I wish we could take more of the credit, but this was only half on us," one of the mercenaries admitted. "These bad boys you smuggled for us did as much work as we did."

"For sure," another agreed. "These rifles don't mess around. They blasted through those armored soldiers like it was nothing."

They held up the Elm-made bolt-action rifles they were carrying.

"How'd you even get your hands on these?"

Masato replied with a light shrug. "I was the angel in charge of all Elm's logistics, remember? It was a piece of cake."

Due to the sheer scale of the flow of goods, Masato had known that the Bluebloods were assembling a gigantic army. If he hoped to successfully protect Neuro, he had to be capable of outmatching that force with a much smaller one. That was why, before he left Elm, Masato secretly diverted some machinery and equipment to Lakan and poached a fully trained Elm engineer. In a world where flint-lock weapons had yet to achieve widespread adoption, the power that bolt-action rifles possessed was hard to overstate.

"Anyhow, me and the grandmaster still have some stuff we need to hash out, so you guys are dismissed for the day. Just remember, it won't be long before we see more action, so make sure you don't drink yourselves *too* stupid."

""""Yes sir!"""""

When Masato dismissed them, the mercenaries dispersed through the city.

Neuro strolled over as though to take their place. "I have to say, those are some well-trained men you've got. Color me green with envy."

"That there's the Qinglong Gang, the biggest mercenary company in Lakan. Their skills are no joke. Lakan's got a double-digit number of powerful families who spend all their time secretly warring for control, so the mercs get to build up loads of experience."

"Perhaps not for much longer, however. I hear that the infighting settled down a great deal when Shenmei Li officially became chancellor. And I've *also* caught wind that you played a big role in the ousting of her predecessor. I must say, I never took you for such a Lakan man."

"The flow of goods made it obvious that the Bluebloods were about to stage a coup. You're my ticket home, and if I wanted to keep you alive and kickin', I needed some troops I could deploy as I pleased. Lakan was the best place to get 'em. That's all there was to it."

The Freyjagard Empire had been an aristocracy for ages, and in an aristocracy, you earned followers with prestige. The problem was, lineage and notoriety weren't the kinds of things that could be obtained overnight.

However, the Lakan Archipelago was different. True to its name, it was a collective body of islands each ruled by a different family. This made their national bonds far weaker, and prestige carried little luster there. Instead, Lakan culture valued wealth, something far easier to acquire in a hurry than reputation—especially for a prodigy businessman like Masato Sanada.

That was the true reason he'd gone to the Lakan Archipelago instead of heading straight for Freyjagard.

"So you earned the new chancellor's trust to ensure that she'd announce the Lakan Archipelago's support for the Four Grandmasters in the Freyjagard civil war and all so I'd owe you one."

"I scratch people's backs, they scratch mine. It's the only way to keep everything even. I'm a merchant, after all. It wouldn't sit right with me if I just took advantage of your goodwill and never gave you anything in return," Masato said with a jaded smile.

Neuro's expression remained congenial…

"But that was all you acting on your own."

...but all of a sudden, he squinted probingly.

"As I'm sure you're aware, the rest of your otherworldly friends are making quite a mess for me over in Yamato. I must know, what made you decide to split from them?"

"I told you back when I came offerin' to help, didn't I? I gotta return to my original world, no matter what it takes. You're the only one who knows how to do that, so when Tsukasa started talkin' about makin' moves that might piss you off, I put my foot down and bailed."

Masato gave Neuro's unsubtle scrutiny a simple answer: His interests had fallen out of alignment with the group's. That was all there was to it.

"Why, you afraid I'm a spy or something?" the prodigy businessman pressed. "You already let me and my men into your stronghold; I figured that meant you trusted me at least a *little*."

"Oh, no, I believe you. In fact, I had a front-row seat to your little breakup."

"What?"

This time, it was Masato's turn to give Neuro an inquisitive look.

Neuro responded by letting out a laugh that rocked his shoulders. "Ha-ha-ha. Having it out like that in front of an imperial exchange student was a sloppy move."

"So you used Nio, huh?"

"Not just him. I did a little tampering with all the exchange students we sent over to Elm. I can peer through any of their eyes to view exactly what's going on."

"What are you, a voyeur or something? You seem like a stand-up guy, but you've got some real shady hobbies."

"Didn't I tell you? All I want is to live a peaceful life in this new home of mine, but you and your friends are maniacs. The very notion of remaining unaware of your doings takes years off my life."

Now it all finally made sense to Masato. During the original peace talks, Neuro was the one who'd suggested launching a program for studying abroad so that Elm and Freyjagard could deepen their social and cultural ties. His motivation had only been a desire to spy on the Seven Luminaries.

"And see, Masato, that's why I do trust you."

"Good, then we can—"

"But the thing is, the situation's changed," Neuro cut in. "You remember what Lucy said before he died, don't you? About how the Elm ambassadors attacked a member of Yamato's Freyjagard-acknowledged autonomous government, and how the Resistance managed to take Fort Steadfast? Considering that they're cut off from their leader, Kaguya, it's hard to imagine them making such bold moves all on their own. Plus, the Resistance is practically wasting away. No group like that would be strong enough to seize a stronghold. It's obvious that our Elm ambassador escapees—that is, Tsukasa and your other friends—had a hand in all this."

"..."

"I wanted to get along with you guys, I really did. And war is such a headache. Unfortuantely, as an imperial grandmaster, I can't exactly let what they're doing slide. This stuff jeopardizes my head's place on its shoulders. So given the new situation we're in, I have to ask again. Are you really on my side? Actually, let me put it more bluntly."

Neuro locked eyes with Masato...

"If the need arose...would you kill Tsukasa and the rest of your friends?"

...and put him on the spot.

If things came down to that now-possible scenario, which side would Masato pick?

The young man from Earth didn't so much as flinch. "I told you,

I gotta get back to my original world. No matter what it takes, and no matter what it costs. My employees—my *family*—are waiting for me back there. And besides..."

"Besides, what?"

"This was always how it was gonna end for Tsukasa and me. He wants to find better compromises, I want to take the best option, and the two of 'em can never coexist."

Tsukasa aimed to maximize well-being for as many people as he could, whereas Masato wanted to maximize it for himself and the people he cared about. The issue wasn't that one of them was wrong and the other was right. Rather, each of them had a dream they refused to give up on, and those two aspirations were fundamentally incompatible.

Someday, Masato was going to fight Tsukasa and anyone who sided with him.

Thus...

"All this did was speed up the inevitable."

...Masato was ready.

He'd been prepared for a long, long time, having made his peace the day Tsukasa chose to kill his own father and live as a politician.

"Well, all righty then. And it looks like you mean it, too."

Neuro's expression softened upon hearing Masato's answer...

Snap.

...and he snapped his fingers.

The evening sunbeams had stretched Masato's shadow out wide, and a large splash sent ripples through it.

"What the?!"

Arf! Arf!

A large black dog emerged from the shadows. After barking, the creature ran to Neuro and circled him affectionately.

"Who's a good boy?" Neuro said as he petted the dog's head. It dived happily into Neuro's shadow and disappeared.

"What the hell was that thing?"

"You can think of him as a familiar of mine. His specialty is sniffing out lies, so I had him hide in your shadow and told him to rip you to shreds if you tried to pull one over on me."

"You piece of shit..."

Rage flashed across Masato's face at Neuro's egregious precaution. However, Neuro didn't look ashamed in the slightest. "Come on, now, don't give me that scary look. I offered you and your friends an olive branch in good faith, and you stabbed me in the back for my trouble. Can you really blame me for being suspicious? I think a little security is well within my rights. But now I can genuinely put my faith in you. And I do love trusting people. Your bloodlust is authentic. I gotta say, you're one ruthless dude."

"........."

"So come on, there's no need for scowls. It won't happen again, I promise. All right, like I told you before, activating a gate between worlds is a pretty serious bit of magic, so it'll take me some time to get it up and running. I've been making all the necessary preparations down below the grandmaster's estate, but it'll still require three more months to complete. If you agree to ally with me until it's ready, I promise I can get you home. Do we have a deal?"

"Yeah. It's a deal." Masato had a couple of questions and doubts, but at the moment, Neuro was his only way back to Earth. Instead of offering any complaints, he nodded in acceptance. "In that case, now that we're back to trusting each other, I've got a question. What's our next move? Heading over to Yamato to put down the rebellion?"

Neuro shook his head. "Nah, that ship has sailed. I don't know when exactly it was that Fort Steadfast fell, but information travels slow in this world. Even if word traveled by the swiftest dragon, it'd still be three or four days before the news reached *Lucy*."

Magic for telepathic communication did exist, but it only worked at short ranges. More importantly, all the mages except Neuro who could use spells that advanced were off conquering the New World with Lindworm.

"If you add in the ten days or so it must've taken the Bluebloods to coordinate their revolt all across the empire simultaneously, we're looking at an event that happened at least two weeks ago," Neuro explained. "I find it exceedingly hard to imagine that Tsukasa's been spending his time since then twiddling his thumbs in that fort. I imagine the conflict in Yamato has progressed considerably."

"Yeah, that all checks out."

"Even if we try to get involved now, everything we do will be late. I'd just as soon avoid getting played for a fool. What's more, the fact that Tsukasa and his friends took *her* along means they've got an idea of Yamato's situation. I don't know for the life of me how they figured it out, but they did."

Neuro suddenly frowned in frustration, but Masato didn't have the context he needed to understand the meaning behind the expression. Cocking his head, he asked, "What?"

"Oh, don't mind me," Neuro replied evasively. "For now, we need to focus on stamping out the Bluebloods' efforts in the empire. Gotta secure the home front first, or it'll be hard to get anything done. I'll be counting on you."

Neuro thumped Masato on the shoulder. His cloak fluttered behind him as he headed back inside the estate.

"Teacher…?"

The moment Neuro disappeared from view, Masato heard a voice timidly call to him from behind. He turned around to find Roo, the *byuma* slave girl he'd bought in Dormundt, with worry swimming in her eyes.

"Are we gonna have to fight everyone?"

"…Depends on how things shake out, but maybe, yeah."

"Are you really okay with that?"

"I mean, I'd rather avoid it, if we can," Masato admitted. "But at the end of the day...it's like I told Neuro. Eventually, Tsukasa and I are gonna have to settle the score. That's just the way fate shook out for us. Y'see, Li'l Roo, people like you and me are never gonna get on board with that fair and equal world he's after, or the universal basic income he's gonna have to set to get there. I've known that for a while now... and I'm pretty sure he has, too."

Masato paused.

"Also, Tsukasa and I aren't the only ones in play here."

"Huh?"

"I'm sure Ringo and Prince'll stick with Tsukasa to the bitter end no matter what, but the other three are different. Shinobu, Aoi, and Dr. Keine are only working with him 'cause their interests happen to be aligned at the moment, that's all. Each of 'em has their own brand of righteousness, and there's no guarantee that what they think is correct and what Tsukasa does are gonna be compatible forever."

Shinobu Sarutobi was a journalist, and her actions didn't always serve the designs of Tsukasa and his administration.

There were times politicians had no choice but to play nice with people they didn't agree with, but whenever that fact came to light, it was often difficult to get their constituents to understand why they'd done so.

Then, there was Aoi Ichijou, and she and Tsukasa were already on somewhat dubious terms. The thing was, Aoi didn't always fight for the side the Japanese government preferred. The United States was a close ally of Japan's, yet its military had found itself on the receiving end of Aoi's blade a few times, and her actions had caused more than several diplomatic incidents for Japan.

Finally, there was Keine Kanzaki. The way Masato saw it, Keine was in the same boat as he was. Eventually, she and Tsukasa were going to have to part ways for good.

©Sacraneco

Masato's intelligence network on Earth had kept him abreast of events across the world, both in public and behind the scenes. Through it, he'd learned of the deeply unethical practices Keine employed on the battlefield. Her moral philosophy vastly differed from society's. Masato couldn't begin to make heads or tails of it, but given how highly Tsukasa valued human rights, he likely found her all but repugnant.

"We were always kind of an oddball crew. You've only ever known us as a group, so this might come as a surprise to you, but if not for us crashing here together, you'd never have seen us all workin' as one."

"Roo never knew…"

"Still, I'm not a monster. I'm not just gonna let Ringo and Prince hang out to dry. Even if things turn ugly, I want to at least use my position with Neuro to get him to spare their lives. With things the way they are, though, that's probably as much as I'm gonna be able to do for 'em…" Masato glanced down with a hint of sadness in his eyes. "If you're upset with me after hearing all that, you don't have to keep tagging along."

"Roo would never leave!" The little girl shouted at the top of her lungs. "You bought Roo as a slave, and Roo is gonna stay right here! Roo's gotta learn lots more stuff from you to buy her mommy and daddy back!" she declared.

"Well, all righty then," Masato replied, grinning.

Roo stuck to her contracts, and she was honest and direct about what she valued. Both of those were admirable qualities for a merchant to have.

"That's what I like to hear. Remember, if you don't know what you want, you'll never get anywhere."

The young girl's eyes never strayed from their target, and nothing was going to sway her. With the kinds of talents she possessed, it wouldn't be long before she made that dream of hers a reality.

And that would only be the beginning.

Once Roo realized the power she had at her disposal, she wouldn't be able to help herself from testing its limits, just as Masato had.

I've got dreams and desires of my own to fulfill.

Masato turned his gaze to the eastern sky and his thoughts to his age-old foe who waited somewhere in that direction.

Excitement welled up in his chest.

CHAPTER 8

❧ Smoldering Embers ❧

It was about half a month before the Bluebloods would stage their coup d'état in the empire.

The Yamato self-governing dominion sat at the easternmost side of the Freyjagard Empire. Its capital, Azuchi, was surrounded on three sides by forested mountains, providing the city with substantial natural fortification. The only way to march from the empire to Azuchi was to go through the Amagi Pass, and the entrance to the mountain range was guarded by the sturdy Fort Steadfast. Throughout Yamato's long history, the garrison had thwarted the Freyjagard Empire's numerous invasions, providing Yamato with opportunities to turn the tides. The fort was downright impenetrable, and for the dominion government, it served as their final line of defense.

Or it had, up until a few days ago. The Resistance, with the help of the High School Prodigies, who'd come to Yamato as ambassadors from the Republic of Elm, had claimed Fort Steadfast as theirs.

"Whoa, the repair efforts are coming along nicely. You've got that wall we blasted nearly completely patched up."

"Darn tootin' I do. I'll have you know I'm a professional."

"Wait, you're a carpenter? I coulda sworn you were a winter hunter like me."

"Okay, technically it was my old man who was the carpenter."

"That makes you just as much an amateur as the rest of us, pal."

"Hey, I've been helping my dad out with his work since I was a kid. Even after I became a winter hunter, I always handled all the repairs 'n' stuff when we made camp. As you can see, I've still got it." As he spoke, the *byuma* who'd been restoring the section of the fort that got destroyed in battle the other day took a breather. He sat down on a pile of rubble and drank from his canteen. "Ah, that hits the spot. Course, if they'd sent me some of the guys makin' that *weird doohickey* inside, I coulda finished even quicker. I guess it's fine, though. The wall wasn't too busted up to begin with."

"True." The other Resistance member, a skinny *hyuma*, nodded in agreement. "Makes sense, what with how quick our siege ended. Never thought I'd see Fort Steadfast fall that easy."

"It's all thanks to Ms. Aoi. I can slash through iron, too, but the most I can manage is about three bu [just under half an inch]. I can't believe anyone other than Master Shishi is capable of cleaving through Fort Steadfast's ten-sun-thick [about twelve inches] iron gate with just a sword."

The two of them turned and glanced over at Fort Steadfast's entrance.

The garrison had only one entrance, which had once been barred by a twelve-inch-thick iron gate that was substantially sturdier than the stone walls encircling Fort Steadfast. However, the gate was a shadow of its former self now. It had been sliced into seven slabs of iron, and prodigy inventor Ringo Ooshi was hard at work trying to join them back together.

The Resistance had stormed Fort Steadfast a few nights prior, and the first step of their raid had been for prodigy swordmaster Aoi

Ichijou to intentionally cleave through the sturdiest part of the structure as if slicing through tofu.

It made for an awe-inspiring sight—one that the Resistance fighters would never forget. Nor would they ever fail to recall the shrill screams that had risen up from the enemy combatants inside.

"Guess ya can't blame 'em for freaking out when we charged in that boldly."

"You can say that again. Those angels were a godsend for sure, but we pulled our weight, too. Fort Steadfast's stopped tons of imperial invasions, but we took it over in a single night with basically no losses. We're pretty dang strong."

"Don't go gettin' big head., ."

""!!""

The newcomer hadn't so much as raised his voice, but his words struck the pair of soldiers as surely as if they'd been shouted. They turned around…

"C-Commander Kokubu!"

…and saw a man standing behind them. It was the middle-aged, suntanned samurai who'd given orders during the attack on the fort. He was a longtime veteran and, after Shura, the second strongest member of the Resistance forces.

Kokubu turned his sharp, hawkish gaze upon the two young soldiers drunk on the taste of the victory. "You kids did good work, sure, but we only got through the battle so painlessly because of Mr. Tsukasa."

"Really?"

"While Ms. Aoi distracted our foes, he set up barrel bombs at the fortress's rear wall and blasted a hole in it. But instead of using the opening to invade, he abandoned it to rejoin Ms. Aoi. Didn't that strike you as odd?"

"It did," answered one of the two warriors. "I wondered why

bother going through the effort to make an entrance he wasn't gonna use. All it did was leave more for us to clean up."

Kokubu shook his head. "It might've seemed meaningless, but that there was the most critical maneuver of the whole battle."

"How so?"

"By giving our opponents an escape route, Mr. Tsukasa prevented the fort's soldiers from becoming dead men walking."

In military parlance, this was known as a three-sided siege. When you attacked an opponent, boxing them in on all four sides and leaving them no way to retreat would drive them to desperation and turn them into dead men walking—soldiers who could no longer be cowed by the fear of death. That kind of abandon paved the way for a vicious counterattack, and the phrase "three-sided siege" was a reminder to always leave one side open. No matter the era, keen military leaders were careful never to attack every gate when they were assaulting a castle. Standard operating procedure was to make sure your enemies had a way to flee so they didn't become cornered rats.

However, that necessary tactic proved difficult to employ because of Fort Steadfast's construction.

The bastion possessed only a single gate for entrance or exit. What's more, it was incredibly heavy and made of iron, so it wasn't the kind of thing someone could open on a whim. Fort Steadfast was designed that way precisely because it was the Yamato capital's final line of defense. Just as the doctrine of three-sided sieges asserted, the best way to draw out a soldier's full strength was to turn them into a dead man walking, and Fort Steadfast was designed specifically to prevent the people defending it from fleeing. By taking advantage of that psychological mechanism, the garrison drew the most out of every soldier defending it. While the dead men walking held back their enemy's advance with their newfound tenacity, reinforcements from Azuchi could circle around the enemy army and launch a counterattack.

It wasn't mere luck that had allowed Fort Steadfast to repel the imperial army on so many occasions. Every miracle had some trick or contrivance behind it, and that no-escape-method had allowed Yamato to overcome many crises since the nation's founding. That cruelly rational system was the bastion's foundation, the source of its strength and impregnability.

Naturally, attacking Fort Steadfast without accounting for that factor would have led them to tremendous losses. A single glance at the structure's location and layout had been enough for Tsukasa to recognize that.

That was why he'd turned the whole situation on its head.

By loudly destroying the front gate and stirring up the enemy troops' fears, then blowing a hole in the outer wall right when they thought there was no escape, Tsukasa had offered the defending Yamato forces a way out. As they grappled with the notion that they would die, Tsukasa offered them a single ray of hope to latch on to like a proverbial spider's thread being lowered into the depths of hell.

There wasn't a person alive capable of refusing that lifeline.

With that, Fort Steadfast became little more than an antiquated pile of rocks.

"The soldiers in Fort Steadfast fled in fear of Ms. Aoi's might, and that allowed what should've been a protracted siege to end in a single night. Now we control a forward outpost in our campaign to take back Yamato, and it hardly cost us a man to achieve it. Who cares about slaughtering the fort's soldiers when we already got the biggest prize there is?"

The two younger soldiers gave their commander's explanation a pair of appreciative nods.

"O-oh, wow… So that's what happened…"

"I get it. We cut through that thick gate instead of goin' in the side to make our foes feel like they didn't have a shot."

The two of them had been on the breaching squad and had witnessed firsthand just how unmotivated the fort's defenders were. It was all thanks to Tsukasa's plan that eliminated what made Fort Steadfast so steadfast before his side ever set foot in the structure.

That wasn't all, though. There was something else that made Commander Kokubu confident that Tsukasa deserved the credit for the plan's success—the responses to his orders during the attack.

"Listen... Remember how Mr. Tsukasa personally went through each of our squads and shuffled the members around before the attack? Well, his reorganization was nothin' short of incredible. I was an officer during our last big war with Freyjagard, too, and in all my days, I'd never commanded squads anywhere near as coordinated as the ones we had the other night."

The group in charge of blasting the wall got it done without a hitch, those meant to storm the garrison ran in gallantly without hesitation, and the squad responsible for covering the flank did so with an almost paranoid level of vigilance.

Everyone had executed their tasks beautifully.

It sounded so easy, but in most battles, achieving that level of control was a pipe dream. Yet the inexplicable had been a reality this time.

"Most of the Resistance troops are like you boys and only became soldiers when they got conscripted in the war three years back. Goes without saying that none of you have the experience of proper fighters. Yet your precision, your speed, everything you did put our seasoned enemies to shame. And the only reason that was possible was because every one of you fit your assigned roles like a glove."

"So you're saying that Mr. Tsukasa figured out what each of us was good at and appointed us to squads where we could do our best?" the *hyuma* soldier asked.

"Th-there's no way. He must've just gotten lucky, right?" the *byuma* said.

Kokubu answered their questions with one of his own. "You ever tell Mr. Tsukasa you were good at carpentry?"

"Who, me? No, I don't think so. During the reorganization, I told him about me being a winter hunter, but… Wait, huh?" The *byuma* soldier gasped. "Hey, you're right. I never mentioned carpentry once."

Kokubu had hit the nail on the head. Sure enough, Tsukasa had determined the individual talents of Resistance members he'd only just met and put them into suitable groups. Being prime minister required delegating responsibiliteis to huge numbers of people, and it was in that role that Tsukasa had fostered his keen powers of observation. Everything about a person's appearance, from the way their gaze shifted, to the movements of their mouth, to how tan their skin was, to the state of their hands, to their build, to the length of their fingernails, and even to the odor they gave off, told the story of their life.

Tsukasa saw all of it.

He discerned people's emotional states from their actions and gestures, and by inspecting their physiques, he could intuit the processes by which they'd attained them. Once he was armed with that knowledge, he could pick those best suited for a task. On a large scale, this allowed him to get an organization operating at peak efficiency.

If not for that, he never would have been able to take Japan as it reeled from both a global financial crisis and the previous administration's misgovernance and right the ship in just a single year.

However, the Resistance members knew nothing of Tsukasa's history, so they had no problem interpreting his triumph as that of a supernatural being—an angel.

"Those angel eyes of his can see right through humans like us," Kokubu said. "I gotta hand it to Lady Kaguya. These reinforcements she sent us are somethin' else."

"…You really believe the angels are *actual* angels, Commander?"

"Do you not?"

"I mean, there's no mistakin' how incredible they are, but...they look so human, and besides, I don't know if angels even exist at all."

The middle-aged commander nodded sagely. "Far as I'm concerned, it don't much matter one way or the other." He paused a beat, then went on. "Honestly, I almost hope they *are* human."

"You do?"

"Yeah, maybe. If it turns out that Mr. Tsukasa's power to manage people ain't divine, and he's just a man like you or me, then he must surely be the king of some nation at least a dozen times bigger 'n Freyjagard. I can't for the life of me think of anyone I'd rather have on my side than that."

Prodigy politician Tsukasa Mikogami.

Prodigy inventor Ringo Oohoshi.

Prodigy swordmaster Aoi Ichijou.

The three of them, together with Lyrule, had come to Yamato with two goals.

One of them was to see whether Kaguya, who was still held in the Republic of Elm, was telling the truth about the Yamato people being subjected to inhumane conditions.

The other was to hopefully determine the identity of the "Evil Dragon."

An entity, one that was probably responsible for bringing them to that world in the first place, had once contacted them through Lyrule to deliver a message to them.

"This world...is being engulfed...in a massive evil dragon's maw... I beg of you, O Seven Heroes, you must save this world."

Then there was the Seven Luminaries' religion that had once been popular on this continent.

"Long ago, seven heroes arrived from another world and saved the continent from an evil dragon's rule."

Based on those two pieces of information, they had already concluded that the evil dragon was some sort of threat to the world. However, its exact nature remained unclear. All Tsukasa and the others knew was that if they returned to Earth via Neuro's magic, the notion of some evil dragon terrorizing this world would haunt them. People of this planet had aided the Prodigies and even saved their lives. And during their time here, the high schoolers had made all sorts of irreplaceable friendships. Regrets were the last thing they wanted to have. If some great danger approached and could only be stopped with their help, then they would do everything they could. Only then would the teenagers be able to head home with clear consciences.

That was why, when Neuro offered to send them home, they'd asked for a postponement instead of immediately accepting. And in the meantime, they'd gotten to work investigating the evil dragon. That was when Princess Kaguya of Yamato told them of a small tribe of elves who lived in her country and told their children, "Yggdra doth not like bad children—and a mean old dragon will gobble them up." The tale bore a striking resemblance to the stories about the evil dragon.

According to Kaguya, the elves lived in a hidden village in Yamato, and the Prodigies figured visiting this secluded place might reveal more about the evil dragon's true nature. Unfortunately, not even Kaguya, who was an elf, knew of the settlement's location. The Prodigies knew that finding it would be no easy task, but it was the first decent lead to pursue. There was no way they were going to give up on it.

Following that tiny thread had brought them to Yamato and had led to their acquiring the journal of a traveling merchant—Elch's father Adel—who they suspected had traveled to the elf village.

A few days had passed since the occupation of Fort Steadfast, and night had fallen.

Up on the ramparts, Tsukasa flipped through an aged journal. It was the one he'd been given by Resistance tactician Kira, the one that had belonged to Adel. Tsukasa suspected that the elves might know who or what the evil dragon was, and this diary was the one present clue to the elf village's location.

A little while had passed since Tsukasa received the journal, but between preparing to capture the fort, overseeing its repairs, and getting ready for the rest of their campaign to retake Yamato, he hadn't been able to set aside any time to read it. Now that the initial reconstruction was done, though, he finally had a few moments to peruse the contents of the account. After quickly but thoroughly reviewing the information contained within…

…Tsukasa let out a long, deep sigh.

Was it out of disappointment?

Not at all.

Adel's notes had simply proved so engrossing that Tsukasa had forgotten to breathe. The writings were of great significance to him and the other Prodigies…

…and to *her*, too.

"Excuse me, Tsukasa?"

"!"

Someone called to the young prime minister standing alone beneath the night sky.

Tsukasa tore his gaze away from the closed journal and looked in the direction of the voice. There he spied *the very girl he'd been thinking of* coming his way. Her long blond hair shone white as it swayed in the moon's glow.

"Hello there, Lyrule. What brings you out so late?"

"Summer's almost over, and if you go out after dark, it brings your temperature down. Especially when it's so windy," she replied, offering Tsukasa a fur blanket.

"Thank you. That was thoughtful." Tsukasa took the quilt and draped it over himself. "You've been treating the wounded, I assume?"

"That's right, and the spirits have been helping me. The time I spent with Keine taught me a lot. Of course, not that many people actually got injured. I have to say, the Resistance's fighters are a sturdy bunch."

"It makes sense. It's been three years since the war, and they've spent that whole time fighting a lonely battle where the very people they're trying to rescue aren't aware they're being dominated. That's the kind of thing that forges hearts and minds alike into steel."

Still, Tsukasa was surprised that the Resistance could muster so many troops, given that the brainwashed people of Yamato saw them as an annoyance. Normally, guerilla tactics were only possible when you had the support of the locals. Without their aid, obtaining supplies became all but impossible, and you would be left to wither away slowly.

However, Yamato's rebellion movement was different.

They were haggard, to be sure, and tired to the bone, but they hadn't let that dull their fangs. Instead of allowing themselves to be reduced to a pack of wild dogs focused only on survival, they had remained as wolves and kept their minds on the real fight.

"I have no doubt they'll be able to retake Yamato," Tsukasa declared. His voice rang with confidence.

Lyrule nodded in agreement, but stopped abruptly. She'd just noticed that Tsukasa was holding Adel's notes.

"Oh, you have Adel's journal. Did you read it all the way through?"

"...I did, yes."

"And, um... What did it say?" Lyrule inquired. Reserved as her voice was, fierce curiosity burned in her eyes.

She wasn't asking if Tsukasa had found information about the elf village. Rather, She hoped to hear Adel's words.

Lyrule had no parents of her own, but Winona was like a mother to her, and with Adel being Winona's husband, he was the closest thing Lyrule had to a father. It was only reasonable for her to want to know what her beloved family member had spent his time doing in this foreign land...and whether or not he'd left any messages for her and the others back in Elm.

The anticipation must have been torturous.

Tsukasa looked down for a moment before answering. "There was a lot. In addition to the journal entries, there were lists of transaction records and sketches of things Adel saw on his travels. There were also a lot of gaps, some of them up to a year long, which makes me think he kept the journal less as a regular habit and more as a way to kill time on long trips. Still, it allows us to track his actions over a fairly long period."

The account detailed how the Orion Company had entrusted Adel with the task of overcoming Yamato's isolationist national policies so it could expand into the new foreign market.

Then it described that Yamato's closed-off topography and general mistrust of the empire led to all of Adel's negotiations going poorly.

Later, midway through his travels, Adel got into an accident after entering a vast forest.

"...One passage explains that when he was at death's door in the woods, he was saved by a small tribe of elves who revered a god named Yggdra...and who believed in a religion called the Seven Luminaries."

Lyrule's eyes went wide. "The Seven Luminaries?! Then...then we were right!"

"We were indeed. We finally found it."

Just as Tsukasa had predicted, the true Seven Luminaries' religion had survived the Freyjagard Empire's purge and continued quietly being practiced deep in the forest of the neighboring nation of Yamato.

"According to Adel's notes, the person who rescued him was Hinowa, Kaguya's mother. This was back before she married into the Yamato imperial family. After that, he began trading with the elf village, and it was actually through Adel that Hinowa and Emperor Gekkou met and became engaged. Both thought very highly of him, and thanks to that, he was able to establish trade routes with Yamato despite their longstanding isolationist policies. Once the Orion Company became the sole pioneers of the Yamato marketplace, it rapidly grew to the largest enterprise north of Drachen."

"I never knew… That must be why Adel refused to turn his back on Yamato in its hour of need."

"Exactly," Tsukasa replied. "The people of Yamato weren't just trading partners to him. In Adel's eyes, he owed them his life. And as for the woods where he had his accident, he doesn't list any precise route, but between his ledger entries and the locations he recorded before and after the incident, I'm certain that it happened in the Forest of No Return in southern Yamato. That alone is a huge find."

A vast sea of trees stretched across the southeastern side of the continent, and somewhere within, there was a hidden elf village.

There, Adel heard the story that went, *"Long ago, seven heroes arrived from another world and saved the continent from an evil dragon's rule."* Later, he'd passed that tale along to Winona.

Finding that hidden village would reveal everything: the story's origin, the nature of the evil dragon, who had summoned the Prodigies, and why. All the secrets would be uncovered at last; Tsukasa was confident after reading Adel's journal.

"Also…" There was one more thing. The diary's contents…contained a big secret about a certain person. Tsukasa hesitated for a moment, but ultimately handed the journal to Lyrule. "There's something else. Some information in this journal concerns you specifically."

Lyrule gasped. "Wh...? M-me?"

"That's right."

"What do you mean?"

Tsukasa shook his head. "I don't think it's really my place to say. Take the diary and read for yourself when you're ready."

It wasn't imperative that Lyrule learn the truth. The events recorded in Adel's account would have no immediate impact on the girl's life, and learning of them might only upset her.

For a moment, Tsukasa had considered not mentioning the topic at all, at least not for the time being. *What's the harm in waiting until the Yamato situation is resolved to tell her?* he'd mused.

However, Tsukasa had quickly changed his mind. It didn't matter what else was going on; he had no right to keep this information from her. Doing so would go against everything he stood for as a person.

Thus, Tsukasa relinquished the journal to Lyrule.

"...Okay."

Lyrule seemed a little daunted before Tsukasa's serious expression, but she took the old book from him regardless.

The rest was up to her.

After handing the journal over, Tsukasa turned his gaze away from Lyrule and toward the southern sky. "The Forest of No Return is to our south-southeast, but there are several checkpoints between here and there, and they're controlled by an adversarial power—Princess Mayoi's dominion government.

"Our first course of action will be to change that. Both to ensure we can conduct our search in peace...and to rescue the Yamato people."

Everything about the Yamato self-governing dominion was twisted and wrong. In the war three years prior, Kaguya's sister Mayoi had betrayed her nation and aided the Freyjagard Empire with their invasion. Then she'd sealed away the Yamato people's memories, ruling as though the takeover had been amicable. At first glance, present-day Yamato appeared peaceful and idyllic…but that was nothing more than a facade. The people had been unjustly robbed of their outrage and sorrow. They were being forced to live a lie. It was a flagrant abuse of human rights, and because the Prodigies were trying to elevate civil liberties to a globally acknowledged norm, the issue became that much more pressing for them.

On top of that, Tsukasa had seen something he couldn't ignore. During the dinner at Azuchi Castle, he'd caught a glimpse of the sheer hatred Mayoi carried for Yamato.

"The only reason I even let them live is 'cause my darling told me I had to be a good ruler. Otherwise, I woulda killed 'em off ages ago."

"That woman is a threat. I don't know what exactly transpired between Mayoi and her homeland, but she *despises this nation and everything in it.*

"The longer she has power over the lives of its people, the more likely it is that something terrible will happen."

Now that Tsukasa and the others understood how dangerous Mayoi was, they were obliged to do something about her. They needed to work together with the Resistance to oust her from power before the worst-case scenario became a reality.

In contrast to Tsukasa's enthusiasm, a look of unease crossed Lyrule's face. "I actually wanted to talk to you about that. I'm certainly all for helping the Yamato people, but…I'm just a little worried about everyone back in Elm. Our opponents saw Aoi fighting in that last battle, so I have to imagine that by now they know that we're helping the Resistance…"

She was concerned that their actions would put the Republic of Elm in an awkward political position.

"I can't say your fears are unfounded," Tsukasa replied.

The idea was that they were helping the Resistance as the Seven Luminaries, not as the Republic of Elm. They could truthfully state that when they went to Azuchi Castle as ambassadors, they'd stuck fast to Elm's policy of fighting only for self-defense and never went on the attack. Furthermore, when Tsukasa informed Elm about the situation in Yamato via satellite, he chose to keep their involvement with the Resistance to the High School Prodigies' inner circle. That information never made it to the general public, so the Republic of Elm could truthfully assert that the Seven Luminaries had made that decision independently.

"However, the empire isn't likely to agree to that so easily."

Tsukasa had set up this situation so that when things in Yamato came to a head, the Republic of Elm and its newly assembled national assembly would have a legitimate excuse to cut ties with the Seven Luminaries. It could declare that the situation was the Seven Luminaries' and the Freyjagard Empire's problem and wash its hands of the whole affair. Unfortunately, that alibi wouldn't actually quell the empire's rage.

Diplomatic relations between the Republic of Elm and the Freyjagard Empire were about to break down in a fundamental way. However...

"At the end of the day, the exact same thing would've happened whether we aided the Resistance or not."

"Huh?"

"As soon as things went south at that dinner party and the dominion government attacked us, there were always going to be repercussions concerning Elm's relationship with the empire. Even if we didn't press the issue, the dominion government leaders would inevitably report back to Freyjagard and claim that we threw the first punch."

"B-but that would be a lie, wouldn't it?"

"Definitely. But when it comes to statecraft, having the truth on your side is far less important than having the biggest voice. In diplomacy, you can get away with anything as long as you say it loudly enough for a long enough time. And because we were going to have to get the situation under control one way or the other, our best option was to start choosing which truths we told to make ourselves look as favorable as possible. 'The dominion government attacked us out of nowhere, so we formed a temporary alliance with the Resistance to keep ourselves safe.'"

From the moment the Yamato dominion government drew steel against Tsukasa and the others at the castle, greater trouble was unavoidable. At the same time, however, that meant there was no need to make an effort to keep the peace. Now that the situation had devolved into open combat, Tsukasa's side could milk it for all it was worth; no more waiting around for enemies to come to them.

"Once Freyjagard takes action, our options will become far more limited, so I want to resolve things in Yamato before they have a chance to act. For the time being, we still have the ability to shove all the blame on the Yamato dominion government and insist that all our actions were taken in the name of legitimate self-defense."

"W-wow, that's really aggressive. I don't know that I would have thought of that..."

"Charging in when your opponent is on the back foot and ensuring that you seize all the ground they're forced to give up is basic diplomacy. Compromise and conciliation don't just spring out of thin air. They can only be fostered once both sides have finished exchanging blows. The dominion government crossed the line first, and I have no intention of handling them gently. The next thing we'll want to do is—"

Suddenly, a sound cut through the night from across the pass, silencing Tsukasa. It was the tolling of a bell, and the noise shook the air as it traveled across the whole length of Yamato.

"That's... That's the bell Kira mentioned, isn't it?"

Tsukasa gave Lyrule's question a nod. "And to think that, at first, all I thought it did was tell the time..."

Now that the bell's ringing had interrupted their conversation, the two of them thought back to their first night with the Resistance.

After they'd agreed to aid the Resistance in the name of the Seven Luminaries, they started discussing how they intended to take Fort Steadfast and what their plans would look like from there. During that conversation, Tsukasa had posed a question to Kira, the tactician managing the Resistance in Kaguya's absence.

"There's something I've been wondering. How did the Resistance members protect their memories from being altered like the rest of the Yamato people's?"

"Did Lady Kaguya not tell you?" Kira asked with a tilt of the head. However, when Tsukasa replied...

"She suggested it would be best if we saw Yamato's situation for ourselves."

...Kira smiled. "I can see that Lady Kaguya has placed a lot of faith in you. Now, before I explain, I should start by telling you how Lady Mayoi is brainwashing the masses. That information happens to be of deep strategic importance. Have you ever heard a bell ringing since you crossed the border and entered Yamato?"

"We have. I recall it chiming after we fled from Azuchi."

Tsukasa was referring to when Shiro, the massive wolf that accompanied Kaguya's retainer Shura, led him and the others to the Resistance hideout. During that journey, the Elm delegation had definitely heard an earthshakingly loud bell.

"The noise itself is the magic Lady Mayoi uses to control Yamato.

Inside Azuchi Castle, next to the main castle tower, there's an abandoned belfry that went unused and unmaintained for so long that the whole thing grew over with moss. It was so ancient that it seemed likely to collapse at any moment. Between that and how much of an eyesore it was, we advised Emperor Gekkou on several occasions to have it demolished and rebuilt. However, we were forbidden from even approaching it. I always found that a bit odd...but as it turned out, there was a good reason for that. The bell housed in that tower is no mere worn-down lump of metal but an ancient magical artifact. If someone with magical aptitude casts their power upon it, they can use its song to command all the native spirits of Yamato and send their spell across the nation."

This wasn't the first time Tsukasa had heard about artifacts. He'd encountered mentions of others while digging through all the books on magic he could find in Heiseraat's mansion to prepare for the battle against Gustav. Artifacts were magical devices used in times of yore that people occasionally dug up. Most were simply wands and cauldrons like the sort Lyrule and other modern-day mages employed, but the rare few were incredibly powerful tools that modern magic couldn't replicate.

"Spirits don't just exist in plants and flowers; they exist in people, too. They make up our bodies, and if you meddle with them, it's possible to manipulate people's minds and memories. Magic like that has the power to devastate nations, and that's why the bell's secret was only passed to those who took Yamato's throne. We had no idea until our homeland fell and Lady Kaguya told us about it. Somehow, though, Lady Mayoi discovered the truth despite not being at the top of the line of succession..."

Kira went on to describe how that had led to Yamato's defeat in the previous war. After disguising herself as Kaguya, Mayoi used the bell to delay Yamato's response to the empire's attack. The effects were devastating.

"I don't know where she learned it, but Lady Mayoi has some incredibly powerful brainwashing magic, and thanks to the bell, she's able to spread and maintain it over the whole of Yamato. There are only two ways for people on Yamato soil to escape its effects. Hibari, would you mind showing them the first one?"

"Of course."

When Kira spoke her name, the young woman sitting next to Tsukasa withdrew an item from her sleeve. It was a red drawstring pouch small enough to fit in the palm of her hand. Inside was a beautiful pink clam. The shell was closed up tight and bound with a lock of black hair.

"Each of these amulets has a strand of the owner's hair inside and is sealed with hair from Lady Kaguya's own head. Lady Kaguya made them for us, and it is by their power that some of the Resistance is kept safe from the bell. However, I take it that you angels don't have anything of the sort."

Tsukasa nodded. "That's right. The only things Princess Kaguya gave us were a wolf whistle and a sword."

"I don't have any protective charm, either," Kira said, "and I imagine the imperial soldiers stationed in Yamato don't. Yet the brainwashing still doesn't affect us, and that's because of the second method. It's actually more of a prerequisite than something intentionally achievable, and it has to do with the circumstances of our birth."

"What do you mean?"

"According to Lady Kaguya, the bell only works on the spirits native to Yamato, so while it influences people who've spent generations drinking Yamato water and growing up here, it has no sway over those without Yamato's native spirits in them, like you angels or the imperial soldiers. My parents and I were driven out of Lakan and came to Yamato when I was a child, so the bell doesn't influence me. Most of the Resistance's members are immigrants and people whose families have lived here for three generations or less; all those without strong enough ties to fall under Lady Mayoi's control. After all, Lady Kaguya can only make so many amulets..."

Tsukasa nodded at Kira's explanation.

To sum it all up, the bell was essentially a giant magic wand that could control Yamato's native spirits. However, its very existence gave rise to another concern.

"...That's a dangerous object to have lying around. Given how the secret's been passed down through the generations, it stands to reason that there might have been rulers other than Mayoi who used the bell for selfish ends. Even if you manage to reclaim Yamato from Freyjagard, what's to stop Princess Kaguya from using the bell to bring everyone under *her* control? Don't you find the prospect worrisome?" Tsukasa looked at Kira and Hibari. The two of them had the expressions of pigeons who'd been shot with peashooters. "What's the matter?"

Kira shook his head. "I, um, I don't really know how to put it..."

"You just made me realize that I'd never considered that," Hibari replied.

"...You didn't?"

"No, not at all. Part of it is that before Lady Hinowa joined the bloodline, no one in the imperial family was born a mage, but...more importantly, we just *know*. We've had a lot of emperors across our history, and none of them have ever been the sort to do something so selfish."

Hibari went on to elaborate on the myriad ways the past rulers of Yamato had put their people first. She detailed how they were the first ones to practice what they preached about moderation when times were lean, how they never covered up crimes committed by their relatives and always saw that justice was done, and how none of them had wielded their power to live in luxury as imperial nobles did.

The way Hibari described it, Yamato's emperors acted on behalf of their nation and people without fail. They were ever their own harshest critics, and when it was impossible to spare the citizens from suffering, they made sure to share that burden.

"And Lady Kaguya is no different."

Her people wanted their nation back, and to that end, she had unflinchingly allowed Elm to take her captive. Considering how Elm and Freyjagard were allies, she had to know that an executioner's block might await her. Yet she still hadn't hesitated.

Hibari explained that there was an absolute truth shared by all residents of Yamato, regardless of whether they came from a family that had lived here for generations or were fresh immigrants like Kira.

"Lady Kaguya and Lord Gekkou never wielded their authority against us, instead using their words and deeds for the good of all. And from what I hear, the emperors and imperial families of generations past all did the same. That's why, for the past three hundred years, as far back as our records go, Yamato has never seen an uprising or civil war. If we can't believe in the people who've governed us so justly, what in the world *can* we believe in?"

Hibari's unshakable confidence was plain in her smile and voice, and it was accompanied by the great pride she felt at getting to serve her nation and ruler.

Upon seeing how she beamed, Tsukasa could say nothing but "I see." He was ashamed of himself for having voiced his cynical notion.

Yamato wasn't an island nation but one of multiple counties that all sat on the same continent. Isolationist national policies notwithstanding, the fact that Yamato was situated directly adjacent to the Freyjagard Empire meant there was no way it could stop immigrants from flowing in. Brainwashing that only worked on people who'd been there for generations was an unsustainable way to hold such a population together.

That newcomers like Kira took up arms in Yamato's defense was proof that the nation's previous rulers had fostered positive relationships with their subjects and avoided abusing their power.

"Forgive me. I can see my suspicions were unfounded," Tsukasa apologized to Kira and Hibari. Then he returned to the topic at hand. "Given how much trust your leaders have been able to garner, I clearly have a lot to learn from them once all this is over. More to the point, I understand how Mayoi managed to seize control of Yamato now. I suppose that means our goal is to take out that bell."

Kira nodded. "That's right. Without that artifact's influence over the native spirits, she won't be able to maintain her brainwashing. Basically, destroying that bell..."

"...will dispel the mind control, and the Yamato citizens will recover their lost memories," Tsukasa replied, finishing Kira's sentence for him.

"Precisely. Eradicating the bell is the key to our victory."

As Tsukasa thought back to his first meeting with the Resistance, he glared up at the eastern sky. Tolls yet echoed through the air. "If we can get rid of that artifact, the people of Yamato will be free, and things will return to how they were. The problem is the bell's location. It's located in the heart of Yamato, deep within Azuchi Castle. Mayoi and Jade know that protecting it is a matter of life and death for them, so they'll spare no effort in its defense."

"Will we even be able to reach it with it so heavily defended?" Lyrule wondered.

Tsukasa shook his head. "Not as things stand, no. The Resistance's full forces number seven hundred strong, but only a hair over a hundred are ready to fight right this instant. In contrast, our intelligence suggests that, including all the imperial forces, the Yamato army is composed of over five thousand soldiers. We're grossly outnumbered, and our foes are better equipped, to boot. And to top it all off…there's the matter of that white-faced samurai, Shishi."

On their way back from their peace accord with Neuro, the Seven Luminaries' envoy group was beset by an imperial noble and his band of knights. Shishi, a *byuma* samurai wearing white powder and red *kumadori* makeup, was one of the assailants. He was the father of Kaguya's retainer Shura, the White Wolf Genreal. Shishi had proved strong enough to overpower Aoi in single combat. The prodigy swordswoman had been wielding an inferior sword at the time, but her loss was still a shock.

Shishi was the enemy's wild card. Even operating as a solo fighter, he was mighty enough to shape this entire war.

Ignoring the threat he posed would be folly.

"According to Princess Kaguya, he was only on temporary transfer to the empire to serve as a sword instructor at the time. Normally, he leads the Yamato dominion army. His being away when we fled the castle was a stroke of good fortune for us, but I wouldn't be surprised to learn that he's returned in the interim. Regardless of whether he was in Freyjagard during our escape, Mayoi and Jade almost certainly called him back afterward out of fear that the Republic of Elm would retaliate for what they did. There's no sense in holding onto false hope. We should assume Shishi is here and plan accordingly."

With that being the case, any plan that relied on Aoi brute-forcing her way through enemy lines was off the table. The situation was stacked pretty heavily against the Resistance.

"If we want to *prevail in spite of that*, then we're going to need to get crafty."

With that, Tsukasa pulled his eyes from the eastern sky, peering at the solid ground below. Following his gaze, Lyrule noticed something. Fort Steadfast shone white under the argent moonlight from atop its perch on a gentle slope. A swarm of shadowed figures steadily approached from across the rugged terrain.

"Are they who I think they are?!"

"That's right. They're exactly who we've been waiting for."

It wasn't the enemy. No proper army would ever move in such a scattered formation.

No, the group headed to Fort Steadfast under cover of night worked diligently to seemingly bolster the Resistance's meager forces.

"The people we're fighting against are innocents who've had their memories tampered with, so we want to keep casualties on both sides to an absolute minimum. Our goal is to secure the most victories with as little fighting as possible. We need to start by dealing with the elephant in the room and shrinking the difference between our total forces and the enemy's. If we're lucky, seeing what we're up to will make our opponents panic and bait them into an ill-conceived siege. Let's see how this plays out."

As it turned out, Tsukasa's prediction was right on the mark.

That very day, Yamato's Samurai General, Shishi, returned to Azuchi from his stint training Archduke Weltenbruger's Shwarzrichtenritter in the art of swordsmanship.

"Master Shishi! Welcome home!"

"It's so good to have you back!"

It was said that all of Yamato's samurai could slice through iron like it was nothing, but there was one man in particular whose overwhelming strength was without peer. The soldiers celebrated his return with joyous cheers.

"You have no idea what a relief it is to have you here with us, sir!

A few days ago, the Resistance and their Elm angel collaborators took Fort Steadfast as part of their grudge against our good friends in Freyjagard..."

"So I've heard," Shishi replied. "Where is the administrator? I need to discuss our response with him immediately."

"I believe he's in the keep with Lady Mayoi," one of the castle guards replied.

"Very well."

Having learned of Jade's location, Shishi headed straight for the keep.

"You useless little SHIT!"

"Agh! I'm sor—! Ahhh!"

When Shishi reached the top of the stairs, he heard a man throwing a temper tantrum, a woman's muffled screams, and the sound of flesh being struck repeatedly.

Shishi took off at a run, speeding down the hallway, and hurled open the sliding door to the room where the noise was coming from.

"This! Is! The! Worst! Why'd those shitbird angels have to go and make such a giant mess, huh?! When Archduke Weltenbruger finds out we lost Fort Steadfast, all that goodwill I earned by stabbing the grandmaster in the back is gonna go flying out the window! And it's all because you couldn't keep your *goddamn mouth shut* for ONE lousy dinner party, you stupid bitch!"

"*Kaff, koff!* I'm s-so sorry. Ow! I'm sor—"

Inside, Shishi found Administrator Jade von Saint-Germain standing with a look of rage over Mayoi, who was curled up on the floor, desperately trying to weather his abuse. But that wasn't all—two dead samurai were lying in a massive pool of blood that permeated the room's tatami flooring.

Shishi couldn't begin to imagine how long Jade had been on this latest rampage.

Underneath her disheveled clothes, Mayoi's skin was covered in bruises, and the bandages over the as-of-yet-unhealed wound from her amputated ear were soaked red with blood.

Upon seeing that, Shishi acted.

"——!"

Jade stopped his violence at once.

And he had a good reason—Shishi had just drawn Shoutou Ounin, his blade forged by the same smith who'd made Shura's Shoutou Byakuran, and slid it right up against Jade's throat. The weapon glowed like a firefly as Shishi spoke dispassionately. "Mr. Administrator, I would appreciate it if you cooled your head."

"So the big lug is back." Jade gave Shishi a deranged, bloodshot glare and pointed at his sword. "What's the idea here, huh? You gonna kill me? Is that it? You're gonna kill the only reason your oh-so-precious Mayo-Mayo has for living? Hey, uh, word to Mayo-Mayo. Ol' Shishi here is trying to off your squeeze, in case you hadn't noticed. You good with that? Damn, girl, that's cold. And here I thought you actually *loved* me."

The moment Jade questioned her love for him, Mayoi's entire body quivered.

She was terrified of losing her one and only beloved.

While remaining prostrated on the ground, she raised her head and began screaming as she vomited from the pain in her guts. "*Kaff, koff!* Get your filthy hands off him, you worthless lunk! Then go die! Just die already, okay?!"

Although Shishi had just swooped in and saved her, Mayoi spat contemptuous words at him.

The moment she did, the black crystal embedded in her abdomen flashed...

"........."

...yet *unlike the two dead samurai on the floor*, Shishi made no attempt to end his own life.

He simply lowered his blade from Jade's neck…

"I have been made aware that the insurgents took Fort Steadfast. I wish to discuss our response."

…and got down to business.

Upon being faced with Shishi's undaunted demeanor…

"Tch. *The way Grandmaster Neuro explained it,* Mayo-Mayo's Administrative Authority works even better on strong people with more Yamato blood in 'em. That's some nutty willpower you've got there."

…Jade clicked his tongue and stepped away from Mayoi.

Even he recognized that continuing to lash out wasn't going to help turn things around.

"Eh, whatevs. If you already know the score, that'll make this quick. I'm gonna need you to zip down to Fort Steadfast and slaughter the idiots holed up in there ASAP. Feel free to round up whatever pawns you find lying around to help."

The fort had been seized on Jade's watch, and for him, that made it an emergency. He needed the situation to be dealt with, and Shishi was the man to do it.

However, Shishi wasn't so certain. "Is that not too hasty? Fort Steadfast is a mighty bastion. Attacking it now will cost us a great deal of men."

"Do I look like a guy who gives a shit how many of you Yamato shitstains die? I told you to jump, so the only question I wanna hear is 'how high?'! Besides, none of this woulda happened if you worthless Yamato samurai hadn't let that single damn angel chick make you look like a buncha chumps!"

"About that."

"What?"

"That angel, Aoi, is strong. When last we clashed, she was hindered by a blade that failed to equal her technique. But I'm told now that she has borrowed Byakuran from Shura and has overcome that impediment. Should we challenge her while forgoing our tactical advantages, we stand to suffer tremendous losses."

"Again, I *do not care* how many of you sacks of garbage have to die as long as I—"

"You want to win Archduke Weltenbruger's regard, yes? As the man tasked with overseeing this dominion, do you not think carelessly discarding the lives you manage would reflect poorly on you?"

"Tsk…"

Shishi's argument was enough to end Jade's irritation-fueled rebuttals. In truth, even Jade recognized that quelling the insurrection with as few Yamato deaths as possible would be the optimal outcome for him. Hearing Shishi lay it out like that helped him recover some of his cool. "…What would you have us do then, huh?" he asked. "You got some sorta plan?"

"Our circumstances hardly call for one," Shishi responded simply.

"Say what?"

"The latest news from our scouts holds that our foes are gathering in Fort Steadfast.

"They number just shy of four hundred, but their ranks grow by the day.

"Considering the scope of their past activities, we place their full forces at seven hundred strong.

"Their aim is doubtless to use Fort Steadfast as an outpost to gather their troops at, then attack Azuchi with everything they have. Regardless, they still have but seven hundred fighters. Even counting the women and children, the total scarcely reaches a thousand. Their full strength amounts to nothing more than a paltry force."

In Yamato, even the women and children were nothing to be taken lightly. Their physical abilities far outstripped those of their imperial counterparts, and with access to weapons, many of them were fully capable of fighting.

However, that was no matter.

Most of the dominion's forces were Yamato citizens, too.

In short, Shishi asserted that there was no sense in getting riled up over such a small group of foes. Hastily rushing in would accomplish nothing of benefit.

"The Resistance has no local support. Their supplies are meager. They cannot possibly hold the fort long. Soon enough, they will be forced to come out on their own. I see no need to take the initiative. Not when sieging them would put us at a crushing disadvantage. Instead, we ought to play this by the book, seize a positional advantage, and use our overwhelming numbers to crush their reckless advance."

Their foes were massing, but they were doing so after spending three years on the run. The Resistance's troops were haggard and weak, and the dominion army was as mighty as ever. All the dominion forces needed to do was hold tight and meet the rebels' attack head-on.

Shishi's counsel earned him a glower from Jade. "What kind of positional advantage are we talking about here? I swear, if you tell me you wanna fight them in Azuchi..."

Shishi shook his head. Battling in Azuchi *would* give the dominion army a tactical advantage, but allowing their foes to breach the stronghold was too dangerous. Doing so would leave Jade's forces no room to regroup and recover in the event that something unexpected occurred. That wasn't a problem, however, for Azuchi wasn't the only place where they could secure advantageous footing.

"There are but two routes one can use to bring a large-scale force from Fort Steadfast to Azuchi," Shishi explained. "One is the road on the Amagi Pass that lies between the fort and the capital. The other involves taking a wide detour around the mountains and crossing north over the Oono Plains. Both routes are viable.

"However, we must also consider that our foes took on a good deal of risk capturing Fort Steadfast. I have no doubt that their true intention is the former path—the shortest journey from the fort to Azuchi. Knowing that, I suggest we take all our forces in central Yamato, assemble them in Azuchi, and form an army of four thousand.

"From there, we can garrison a thousand men in Azuchi while taking the other three thousand and forming a defensive line in the Amagi Pass. That will give us the high ground and allow us to pick favorable engagements."

"Oh yeah?" Jade replied. "And what're you gonna do if they ignore the pass and take that detour across the plains, huh?"

"That would be fine, too. The forests surrounding Fort Steadfast make it hard to track our foes' movements, but the Oono Plains are open and exposed. If they marched that way, we would easily spot them, even from atop the pass. In the time it will require them to circle the mountains, we will be able to return to Azuchi ahead of them. We would be forced to react, yes, but our response would be academic. Once we see them crossing the plains, we can split our forces on the pass into two units and have each one take a different route down the mountains. Fifteen hundred soldiers will greet the rebels head-on from the Azuchi side, and the remaining half will pincer them from behind, securing a complete victory."

The primary advantage to controlling Fort Steadfast was its access to the Amagi Pass and the expediency that route provided to Azuchi. Infantry could make the trek in a single day. By contrast, the roundabout journey across the Oono Plains required three days. The Resistance forgoing the swiftest option to the capital and willingly providing their enemy time to surround them would be utter suicide.

"However, all that is immaterial. With Kira leading them, our foes will never move along the Oono Plains."

In other words, all the dominion army needed to concern itself with was the Amagi Pass. That was where the rebels would make their move—Shishi was certain.

"Meanwhile, as we mobilize what soldiers we can quickly muster in central Yamato and block off the pass, we can also call back our forces scattered across rural areas and all but a thousand of those stationed across the old border. That will give us another five thousand men to deploy. If our foes act in haste before our reinforcements arrive, we can use our tactical advantage to crush them. If they give in to their cowardice and continue holing up in the fort, we can wait for the five thousand extra men and siege the fort with truly overwhelming numbers."

"Why bother leaving anyone on the old border at all?" Jade asked. "If we bring those guys in, too, we'll have a full ten thousand to work with. I mean, it's not like Yamato even exists anymore. Who gives a shit about defending its border with the empire?"

Shishi gave his question a shake of the head. "That would be too dangerous."

"How's that?"

"At present, we have little insight into how deep the ties between Princess Kaguya and Elm truly run. If the Elm ambassadors came to Yamato intending to aid the Resistance from the onset, then they may have planned for reinforcements to arrive when the Resistance makes its next move. Alternatively, the Resistance could have warriors sheltered abroad that they now wish to call in.

"With our eight thousand against our foes' projected seven hundred, our advantage is already more than sufficient. Rather than raising that gap by another thousand, I should think it more prudent to ensure we stay vigilant against the possibility of aid for the enemy."

"...Hmm. You've got a point there."

"The plan I have outlined is the surest way for us to exterminate the Resistance while putting our army in as little danger as possible. My goal is to avoid having Yamato come to harm, and yours is to elevate your social standing in Freyjagard. I feel this is a matter we can see eye to eye on. What say you, Administrator?"

Shishi's tone was unemotional, but his tranquility gave him a certain persuasiveness. He'd explained why Jade's plan to storm Fort Steadfast was rash and outlined a better, more efficient way to destroy the Resistance.

Jade gave him a petty glare…

"Ha-ha-ha. Haaaaa-ha-ha-ha!"

…then out of the blue, he burst into laughter.

"Darling?" Mayoi asked.

"Ha-ha-ha! Y'know what, Shishi? You're totally right. That *is* the best way to kill all those poor suckers who are fighting their guts out *for Yamato.* Man… You're not even brainwashed like the others, and here you are, still giving it your all for the dominion government. What a swell samurai general we've got here! You're a true-blue turncoat, you know that? Ha-ha-ha!"

Jade's voice was gleeful, and his words rang with disdain. He was laughing at Shishi for possessing the willpower to shake off Mayoi's mind control and still remain more loyal to her than anyone else. He'd even formulated a strategy to slaughter his old allies.

However, Shishi offered no response to Jade's mockery. He simply waited silently for Jade to accept or reject his strategy.

Jade seemed to find his obedience and the fact that he hadn't said one word in his own defense hilarious, and he gave Shishi a satisfied nod. "All right, I'm in. As Freyjagard admin, I hereby adopt your plan. Go rally those troops and bring 'em up to the Amagi Pass. Just remember, I'm the supreme commander, and you're my loyal lapdog who cuts the fuckers down for me. We clear?"

"We are."

"Good boy. That's what I like to hear."

With that, Jade reached up to thump Shishi on the shoulder—which sat well above Jade's head—and left the room. As supreme commander, he needed to make preparations before he set off for the Amagi Pass.

"Lady Mayoi, are you injured?"

Once Jade was gone, Shishi knelt down and offered his hand to the visibly battered Mayoi. However...

"Get your grubby mitts off me!"

...Mayoi herself slapped it away. It was almost shocking that anyone's expression could contort with such fury.

"Darling, wait up! Wait for me!"

She stood without Shishi's help and tottered unsteadily after Jade.

Shishi was the only one left in the room.

He silently approached the corpses lying on the floor and slid their eyelids shut.

"Bite your tongue. I'm not here to hear you talk."

All of a sudden, the words of loathing his daughter spat at him during their recent reunion surfaced in his mind.

He could still feel her hateful gaze.

Do not waver.

He summoned his willpower and shook off the memory.

"A true-blue turncoat."

From Shura's perspective, that was exactly what Shishi was.

After how drained the last war had left them, though, Shishi knew that the only way for Yamato to survive was under the empire's heel. False as their peace was, they were alive. That was what mattered most.

He was making the right choice.

This was...the only path.

Kira, tactician and interim leader for the Resistance, rushed over to Tsukasa. "Mr. Tsukasa, our recon parties have reported back with news."

It was night, and another few days had passed since they took Fort Steadfast and finished making their repairs.

"Good. Let's hear it."

"First of all, our scouts have news from the Amagi Pass. An enemy regiment left Azuchi early this morning...and it's around three thousand strong!"

Hearing that sent a stir through the nearby Resistance members.

""""T-three thousand...?!"""""

Kira went on. "By the look of things, our enemy is taking all its forces in central Yamato and massing them in Azuchi."

"Does it look like the three thousand soldiers who departed Azuchi are marching to retake the fort?" Tsukasa asked.

Kira shook his head. "No, they stopped their advance the moment they reached the pass. At present, they've formed a defensive formation. The bulk of their forces are infantrymen, and they've only deployed two of the precious Dragon Knights the imperial forces brought with them from Freyjagard. Given that they're setting up ways to trigger rockslides and other traps that make use of the high ground, we can assume that they've given up on Fort Steadfast and are planning to intercept us at the pass."

Tsukasa nodded. "I agree. It sounds like they're hunkering down to hold their position."

According to the intelligence the Resistance had passed along to Tsukasa ahead of time, the imperial troops stationed in Yamato had counted ten Dragon Knights among their ranks. Dragon Knights were nasty opponents, yet the enemy had left the majority of their aerial combatants in Azuchi. If they intended on conducting bombing runs, then it was safe to assume they had no intention of reclaiming Fort Steadfast. Instead, they were purposely holding the Dragon Knights back to guard Azuchi.

It was a clear refusal to relinquish advantage. Tsukasa had to commend the dominion army for the calculated decision.

Even if they had decided to carry out bombing runs, the largest domesticated dragons were only about ten to twelve feet long, and they couldn't transport that much blasting powder at once. Rather than wasting an invaluable air force's efforts on trivial attacks, having them maintain a bird's-eye view of the war situation was far wiser.

In particular, urban warfare had a habit of getting messy, and flying scouts could make all the difference. The remaining eight Dragon Knights could cover the whole of Azuchi. Should the Resistance take the battle to the streets, the dominion forces would be able to track enemy movements with ease. It would be all but impossible for the Resistance to gain the element of surprise.

"It would have made things easier for us if they'd taken all their forces and come at us head-on, but I suppose that was too much to ask for."

Between the defensive lineup on the pass and the Dragon Knights patrolling the enemy base, the dominion army's sensible moves certainly weren't making things easy for the Resistance. When you were working with a smaller army, you won by waiting for your opponent to make a mistake.

"What do our scouts around the fort say?" Tsukasa inquired.

"There are soldiers along the road and stationed at the checkpoints, but no more than there would usually be," Kira replied. "There are also a handful of enemy squads scattered around the fort, but given their small numbers, it appears they're just conducting recon rather than trying to encircle us and starve us out. When our reinforcements arrived at the fort the other day, some of them ran into enemy search teams en route, but when our people fled, the hostiles never gave chase. At no point were any blows actually exchanged."

"They're playing things slow, then. That's not what I like to see."

"What…do you mean?" Ringo asked.

"Due to the guerilla campaign the Resistance has been waging, our foes have a pretty good idea of how large our forces are. The fact of the matter is, we can barely muster seven hundred combatants. The Amagi Pass is the key to this war, and they know that there's no reason to leave it underdefended to support an unnecessary siege. They're keeping an eye on us while also understanding there's no need to keep us from assembling our soldiers. If anything, that's just going to make it easier for them to crush us all in one fell swoop. I imagine that's approximately how they see the situation."

There were only so many routes that could support a full-scale army, so blocking those off was one thing, but trying to stop a small guerilla force from joining up in a country of forests and mountains was an exercise in futility. Any attempt the dominion forces made to do so would demand inordinate time and resources—enough that it would leave their defenses sufficiently thin for the Resistance to punch through. The dominion forces' greed would have been their undoing. A more logical move was to dedicate a small portion of troops to recon and leave it at that.

"Nothing seems to be going our way, does it?" Tsukasa remarked. "Our enemies are refusing to play into our hands. These are the decisions of someone confident and experienced, who knows rushing in is meaningless. Whoever's calling the shots over there, I highly doubt it's Mayoi or Administrator Jade."

"According to our people in Azuchi, Master Shishi returned from his stint with the empire the other day," Kira noted.

"It figures…"

Kira's expression darkened with worry. "The man is a legend. With him commanding the dominion army, it'll take a lot to trip them up. What do we do?"

It was obvious from his face just how anxious he was about facing one of his homeland's greatest heroes. Given the way he clutched his gut, there was a good chance his stomachache had returned. Kira was undoubtedly skilled, but he tended to fixate on the negatives of whatever situation he found himself in.

Tsukasa didn't see that trait of his as a flaw, however. If anything, Kira's timidity was one of his strengths. By constantly imagining the worst possible outcome, he was able to take steps to make sure it never came to pass. The Resistance had survived in hiding for three whole years without falling apart, and that was thanks in huge part to Kira's management.

The man was fine just the way he was.

Forcing himself to act boldly was unnecessary. Not when he was using his timidity correctly and letting it lead him to the prudent course of action. There were as many sets of skills and temperaments in the world as there were people, and everyone had different qualities they brought to the table.

Whatever Kira lacked, the people he worked with could supply.

Knowing that, Tsukasa put an uncharacteristic amount of strength into his rarely used facial muscles and made sure that when he spoke next, it was with an indomitable smile. "Not a thing."

"What?"

"Our opponents are acting strategically, yes, and they're taking all the right steps to make our lives difficult. But the thing is, this all falls well within our expectations. There's no need for us to alter our strategy. From here, we'll continue with stage two and keep massing our forces."

"Through their surveillance net?"

"That won't be a problem. They've already shown that they don't intend on stopping us from gathering, and more importantly, they aren't the only ones with eyes in the sky. Ringo, you're up."

"Y-you got it," Ringo replied, then flipped open the laptop she'd brought with her from Elm.

"What's that...glowing slab?" Kira questioned.

"Think of it as an angelic magical device," Tsukasa replied. "It's linked directly with God Akatsuki's clairvoyance."

Ringo typed away at the keyboard, and the screen changed.

Now it displayed an image taken from the satellite Ringo launched during the People's Revolution to allow the Prodigies to communicate over long distances and direct her nuclear missiles.

"H-how is that possible?! That's...that's a view of Yamato from the sky!"

"With Akatsuki's clairvoyance, we can see our enemies' precise locations and the exact state of their recon operations. Not even the darkest of moonless nights can obscure God's vision."

That earned quite a bit of excitement from Kira and the nearby Resistance members.

"That's... That's incredible..."

"Phew, these angels don't mess around."

"Yamato used to have Dragon Knights of its own, but they all died in the war. Feels good to have air support again."

Despite it being the dead of night, the screen displayed a clear overhead view of the enemy camp, the dominion scouts hiding near shady piles of rocks, and the Dragon Knights giving their mounts rest.

With that clear a picture of where enemies were stationed, there would be no issues executing the strategy Tsukasa had proposed the first day he met up with the Resistance.

The well-thought-out decisions made by enemy command prevented the dominion forces from falling into disarray the way the Resistance had hoped, but Tsukasa was right. Everything was proceeding well within anticipated bounds.

"Ringo, Aoi went over to receive the newcomers. I need you to pass the enemy positions along to her...and tell her that it's time to start setting up that *cannon* inside the fort."

"「「「......！」」」"

"It's finally time, then...?"

Tsukasa gave Kira's question a firm nod. "That's right. The moment they finish setting up that defensive line in the Amagi Pass, we'll move our plan to its final stage. Time is on our opponents' side, however. If we wait around too long, it'll allow them to assemble their forces not just from central Yamato but from the outlying regions as well, and the additional support will let them overrun us.

"If we permit them to gather their full ten thousand soldiers, it'll be game over. Our job is to end this war before their remote reinforcements arrive. It's time to employ *the plan we discussed* to break the dominion army's ranks—then storm Azuchi!"

"「「「＿＿＿＿＿」」」"

"Eep!"

As Ringo operated her laptop, a shiver ran through her entire body. The tension emanating from the nearby Resistance members was palpable.

After listening to Tsukasa's speech, they began trickling away one by one with grim expressions all around.

It was time for them to return to their posts and charges.

Not a single one of them let out a valorous war cry. At this point, they were beyond the need to express their resolve aloud.

They had all spent three years with their homeland and families torn from them. All the while, they ate weeds and wallowed in dirt, barely surviving, yet they *did* survive. Rage and determination burned hot within them, enough to set the sky ablaze.

Heartened by their conviction, Tsukasa fished out his smartphone, launched the messaging app the Prodigies used to communicate with each other...

"........."

...and used his admin privileges to block Masato Sanada from the group chat.

Then he posted a message. This war would have massive repercussions on global affairs, and with that in mind, it was time to lay some groundwork.

"Shinobu, I have a job for you. An urgent one."

CHAPTER 9

⚜ A Nocturnal Counterattack ⚜

The Resistance intended to go through the Amagi Pass to get to Azuchi.

Therefore, it was of the utmost importance that route was sealed off.

Dominion general Shishi had made his case, and after hearing him out, Administrator Jade von Saint-Germain—the man who held all real authority within Yamato—had mobilized troops accordingly, summoning all the soldiers near Azuchi together before setting out from the capital himself. Between the Yamato dominion warriors and the locally stationed imperials, he had a company of three thousand soldiers alongside him.

After leading them near the summit, Jade had them establish a massive defensive line. Specifically, he had the Yamato soldiers set it up. He wasn't foisting off the work simply because it was heavy labor, however. There was a perfectly logical reason for doing so.

Most of Yamato was covered in woods and mountains. Between traps that could trigger rockslides to pitfalls to makeshift fences that would hinder an enemy advance, there was no shortage of ways the terrain could be incorporated into a defensive position. And no people were better suited to setting those ploys than the Yamato natives. The war with the empire had given them lots of experience. Their memories may have been sealed off, but their muscles remembered how to do the work being asked of them.

With astounding skill, they transformed the Amagi Pass into a perfect natural stronghold.

Meanwhile, the imperial soldiers were busy with a task of their own—monitoring the Resistance-controlled Fort Steadfast.

"Hey! Over here!"

It was that time of evening when the sky took on its first hints of vermilion. A scouting party captain waved overhead from the rocky overpass where he'd been observing Fort Steadfast's entrance.

A shadow descended from above at his signal—a dragon with its wings spread wide. It was the Dragon Knight in charge of delivering communications back and forth.

"Yeesh, it's freezing…," the Dragon Knight groaned.

"Yeah, there's not much of summer left. Good work up there," the captain said appreciatively, then offered the Dragon Knight messenger a warm cup of tea he'd brewed.

"Thanks a million. Ohhh, I can feel my fingers again." The Dragon Knight took another leisurely sip, then asked, "So what's the Resistance been up to today?"

"Just as the administrator predicted, they're using Fort Steadfast as an outpost so they can launch an all-out attack," his counterpart replied. "Those punks are swarming like flies. We spotted another two hundred entering the fort just today."

"With the ones already in there, that makes about eight hundred in all, right? Looks like they're finally ready to settle this."

When the dominion forces had first mobilized, Jade had said that given the scale of the Resistance's past attacks, he estimated their ranks at about a thousand if you included noncombatants like women and children, of which at most seven hundred were active combat assets. In other words, the force massing at Fort Steadfast represented a significant percentage of their full head count. They were preparing to deploy everyone they had.

However...

"I don't know why they're even bothering. There's no way in hell a mere eight hundred people are going to get through our army of three thousand when we've set up camp and control the high ground," the captain remarked dismissively.

"Yeah, you can say that again," the Dragon Knight agreed. "And even if they did manage to pull a fast one and slip past us, there's still another thousand soldiers defending Azuchi. If they think they're gettin' inside easy, then they've got another think coming. And while they're tripping over themselves trying to figure out what to do, our main forces can come down from the pass and crush 'em."

"For sure, for sure. And we've got more people coming in, right?"

The Dragon Knight nodded. "Give it a week, and the soldiers from the outlying areas will arrive. It'll take them time to travel to Azuchi, and they've been disarmed as their way of showing allegiance to the empire, but once they're here and all suited up, that'll give us another five thousand to work with. Once that happens, the Resistance is done for."

"Hah. When you put it like that, it almost makes me feel bad for those poor saps holed up in Fort Steadfast. It doesn't matter if they attack or defend; their fates are already sealed. May as well have dug their own graves."

"Heh. That's what those idiots get for going up against the empire." The Dragon Knight scoffed as he climbed onto his mount. "All right, I'm going to report back to headquarters. I'll return at the same time tomorrow, so make sure you keep everything in line."

"Will do. I have to say, though, watch duty is pretty mind-numbing. Are you certain we should continue observing from a distance? Me and my guys'd be happy to kill a few dozen of the bastards on their way to the fort. Hell, we wouldn't even ask for overtime pay."

"Come on, just stick to your orders. Remember, I'm the one who has to report in to Administrator Jade."

Hearing that name reminded the captain of the thin, comically pompous man who'd briefed them all before they departed the capital. "Isn't that guy just some spoiled noble brat?"

"Yeah. Son of a mistress, I hear."

"Ah, that makes sense. I wonder if that's why they stuck him out here in the middle of nowhere?"

"Your guess is as good as mine there, but I'm sure he's got his troubles like the rest of us. The point is, there's nothing Administrator Jade hates more than when things don't go the way he expects 'em to. Even with all those civilians they're bringing in, the Resistance still only has a thousand people at most. Against numbers like ours, they're nothing but dust beneath our feet. We're here to take out the trash, nothing more, and if they want to make our jobs easier by gathering in one place, I say let 'em. Plus, they've got that one nasty piece of work on their side—the one who took on a hundred soldiers back at Azuchi Castle and wiped the floor with them the way Shishi would've. If you want to keep your head attached to your shoulders, I'd recommend you stay put."

"All right, all right, I get it already. I'll keep my head down and do my job. Less work for us, at least."

"Good." The Dragon Knight nodded, then took off into the evening sky, bound for the main camp in the Amagi Pass to relay the scout's information.

After watching him go, the scouting party captain returned his attention to Fort Steadfast in the distance.

What a bunch of idiots.

If they had just gone along with Mayoi's magic, they could have lived out their lives in peace, false though it may have been.

There was no way a revolution that small was ever going to bear fruit. They were going to get crushed, and that was going to be that.

This is going to be the easiest war I ever fought, he mused. And at that moment, there probably wasn't a person in the dominion army who felt differently.

Over the following day, another three hundred gathered under Fort Steadfast's roof. That brought the Resistance's numbers to eleven hundred—a sum slightly larger than the dominion army's initial estimates. However, nobody found that particularly concerning. After all, there were a number of toddlers and elders among the newcomers' ranks. The people of Yamato, *hyuma* and *byuma* alike, were born with considerable physical abilities, so it wasn't as though they were *useless* in a fight, but things were different now than they had been during the conflict with Freyjagard three years before.

This time around, the bulk of their own forces were from Yamato as well, so their foes had no advantage in that regard. And when the dominion reinforcements arrived, and their full army swelled to nine thousand strong, the uptick in the Resistance's ranks would amount to little more than a rounding error. The dominion forces scoffed. Either way, the Resistance was doomed.

Come the following day, something peculiar happened. More support showed up at Fort Steadfast, and they weren't civilians this time. Each was equipped with weapons and armor.

That was enough to earn some frowns.

Now, their enemies had exceeded expectations. Had the Resistance been concealing its strength somehow? Or had they garnered aid from abroad?

The scouts started to get concerned.

By the next day, the situation had worsened. Reinforcements kept arriving.

There weren't *quite* as many of them as there had been the day before, but they were definitely armed and dangerous. Not only did they gather at Fort Steadfast, but it looked like the garrison was at capacity, and some were camping outside.

Something was off. The observing dominion troops were fretting.

Yet again, the Resistance's ranks increased the next day, and the scout party captain found himself struck speechless. His team was beyond mere worry. Their faces were pale as sheets, and they all thought the same thing.

Did we really make the right call?

Was sitting back and letting this happen really the right decision?

Have...have we made a horrible mistake? One that can't be undone?

"What the hell are you talking about?!" Jade roared when the Dragon Knight delivered the news. His face was ghostly pale, and he hoisted the messenger up by the collar. "A-are you sure the scouts weren't just seeing things?!" he demanded, hoping for a different answer.

"I-I'm certain of it, sir!" the Dragon Knight replied. "Ever since they took the fort, the Resistance's ranks have been swelling nonstop! As of today, they're already at over two thousand!"

"There's no fucking way! That's... That's double our projections! What is going on here?!"

Based on the Resistance's previous activities, Shishi had estimated their full size at seven hundred soldiers—or at a thousand, if you included noncombatants. Jade's calculations had supported that conclusion as well. It was inconceivable that the Resistance could maintain a fighting force of two thousand in its current state.

Nothing about this added up.

"W-we suspect they've called in allies from abroad, sir."

A panicked sweat beaded on Jade's forehead. "~~~~~~~!"

Perhaps they'd been sheltering the bulk of their forces outside the Yamato dominion all along, or maybe they'd hired a group of Lakan mercenaries. Worse, the Seven Luminaries' involvement might have inspired Elm to deploy their troops.

Regardless of whoever these unidentified reinforcements were, this was an emergency. The dominion had about three thousand soldiers defending the pass, and now there were two thousand troops at Fort Steadfast. Jade's numbers advantage was crumbling before his eyes.

Shit, shit, shit! Why does nothing ever go the way I need it to?!

He had to do something.

"No way we can let 'em keep bringing in more help. Change of plans! We're taking everyone we've got and slamming Fort Steadfast as hard as—"

"Calm yourself."

"Rrr...!"

Jade glared at the *kumadori* makeup-clad *byuma* who'd just cut him off—Shishi.

Shishi continued, utterly undaunted by Jade's expression. "None of our lookouts on the border have reported anything about reinforcements moving past them. Acting in haste carries grave risks, and our reinforcements from the countryside are only two or three days out. For now, we should continue focusing on gathering intelligence about what our enemies are—"

Hearing Shishi's counterargument turned Jade's face from a panicked shade of white to furious scarlet. "You want us to keep twiddling our goddamn thumbs?! The whole reason we're in this mess is because *you* said that their numbers wouldn't matter even if we sat back and let them gather together!"

Out of nowhere, something slammed into base camp right beside

Jade and Shishi, its heavy landing crushing water barrels and ration boxes.

For a moment, Jade's heart nearly beat out of his chest. Was it an attack? He swiftly realized that wasn't the case, however.

As it turned out, the culprit was none other than a Dragon Knight.

"What the FUCK?! The hell do you think you're doing, riding your dragon right into headquarters?!" Jade bellowed, partly out of anger at having been astonished.

However, the Dragon Knight who'd all but crash-landed had no bandwidth to spare for Jade's temper. He needed to report what he'd seen during his flight. "I come with news!" he shouted, interrupting Jade's rant. "There's some strange activity going on in Fort Steadfast!"

"Wh-what *now*?!"

"Th-they've got a cannon! The Resistance is setting it up in the fort's courtyard, and it's *massive*! It's over sixty feet long and has a ten-foot bore!"

"WHAAAAAAAT?!?!" Jade screamed.

He couldn't help himself. A cannon that long was beyond his conception. How could a weapon that monstrous even exist?

Right as he was about to express this notion…

Oh no.

…he remembered something.

Before the Republic of Elm was formally founded, there was something the Seven Luminaries had deployed to eradicate the Warden of the North, Fastidious Duke Gustav, and his entire massive fortress. Its strike was so mighty that it warped the land's very topography.

"It's the Divine Lightning…"

When Gustav had used his Rage Soleil war magic, God Akatsuki retaliated by bringing down a miracle. Jade had assumed that it operated similarly to magic, but if the miracle's true form was that of a divinely crafted weapon, then that explained the cannon's tremendous size.

After all, it had been powerful enough to blast away a fortress in Gustav from all the way up in Findolph. Its power and range were off the charts, so it stood to reason that everything else about it would defy common sense as well.

The question was, what would happen now that it was set up at Fort Steadfast? Should it be fired…? What then?

The dominion army's defensive line on the Amagi Pass would be annihilated in a single shot. And worse, Azuchi itself was likely within the cannon's firing range. If it was used to bomb the capital…

Noooo, no, no, no, no, no…

Jade would lose everything. All he'd sweated and bled to attain would be meaningless.

That's not an option. No shot.

"You said they're still setting it up, right?! Did it look ready for use?!"

"N-no, sir! From what I saw from on high, the huge barrel was being held up by a series of pulleys hooked to the fort's steeples, and the Resistance was still constructing the platform to fix it in place! I think we have some time before it's operational!"

It was evening, and soon, the sun would set. If the Resistance members were erecting the cannon manually, then their work would inevitably slow after dark.

Marching normally, an army of infantry could make it from the Amagi Pass to Fort Steadfast in about six hours, and if they hurried, they could cut it down to three or four. And given how large the cannon was, there was no way it could be aimed at anything in its immediate vicinity.

If they were going to go, it was now or never.

Jade made the call. "All troops, prepare for battle! We're going to raze that fort before the Divine Lightning is ready!"

Shishi had objections, and he wasted no time in expressing them.

"Hold on. Our foes' actions are baffling in a number of ways. Besides, if they truly do have two thousand holed up in there, then attacking them would put us at an extreme disadvantage. We would be playing right into their—"

However, his voice cut off midsentence—and it was because Jade had just raised his fist and smashed it into Shishi's face. It wasn't enough to so much as make Shishi flinch, but it proved sufficient to quiet him.

Jade glared at Shishi with even more vitriol than before as he shouted, "The only one who's been playing into their hands is you, you brain-dead moron! Look, I get that you're a dumbass bumpkin from the sticks who doesn't know shit, so let me spell it out for you! That Divine Lightning down there? That nasty piece of work is a Seven Luminaries' weapon that only needed a single shot to wipe a fortress the next domain over off the map! It's how they killed Gustav, it's what got Freyjagard to throw in the towel... That cannon basically took down the empire single-fucking-handedly! And like the idiots we were, we gave them time to set it up. Because of YOU!"

"........."

There was a certain amount of truth to that. Shishi offered no rebuttal.

"If you've got such a hard-on for avoiding casualties, then go head up the vanguard. If you want to keep your idiot countrymen alive, storm the damn fort yourself and dice up those Resistance and Seven Luminaries fucks for me! Understand?!"

Jade was no fool. He had the perspective to view situations in their entirety, and he possessed sufficient insight to deduce what made other people tick. That was why he'd accepted Shishi's counsel and deployed his forces atop the Amagi Pass.

Now, though, his eyes were bloodshot. His usual composure was gone.

To him, an attack that could reach Azuchi from Fort Steadfast was utterly unacceptable. There was no getting through to him, and when Shishi recognized that…

"…Very well."

…he agreed to take point on the attack.

"Well, what the hell are you waiting for?!" Jade roared, then turned his reddened face to the two Dragon Knight messengers. "You two, head back to Azuchi and tell everyone who stayed behind to get their asses over here! If they've got horses, they ride. Otherwise, they run as fast as they damn well can!"

"Wh-what sort of formation do you want them to—?"

"We can figure all that stuff out once they get here! Once you're done with the soldiers, join up with the other eight Dragon Knights and return suited up for air raids! Your dragons are fast enough to catch up with us before we make it to the fort, right?! If you're not back in time, it better be 'cause you're *dead*. Do I make myself clear?!"

""Crystal, sir!""

"Then get moving! Hurry it up, or I'll kill you myself!"

Jade kicked one of the dragon's rear ends to urge it on as he began chewing his fingernails and cursing everything happening to him.

"Shit, shit, shit, shit, shit! Like hell I'm going down. Not here!"

The dominion army abandoned their defensive line that stretched across the pass and descended the mountain to march on Fort Steadfast.

Originally, the route connecting Fort Steadfast to the Amagi Pass and Azuchi had been a supply road for transporting soldiers and supplies from the capital to the garrison that was the cornerstone of the city's defense. The path had been designed from the get-go to be used by wagons and large groups, so despite how mountainous it was, the three-thousand-man dominion army was able to hurry down it with ease and clear the mountains before evening turned to night. And they didn't stop there—Fort Steadfast was within their sights, and they surged toward it as a flood.

A great forest stood at the base of the trail, but a large swath of it had been cleared so the supply road could make it from the Amagi Pass to the fort. Nothing obstructed the charge.

Leading the way was Shishi, a *byuma* man whose wolf ears shone white in the moonlight.

As he ran ahead of the army, his expression darkened with anguish.

…Was my judgment in error?

The Resistance had swelled its ranks past what he'd anticipated. At the end of the day, though, that wasn't really a problem. Yamato was surrounded by mountains and woods, and smuggling a small group of people past the border wasn't hard to do, especially with the support of a group like the Resistance. If any rebels stationed abroad or Lakan mercenaries who specialized in guerilla warfare wanted to, they could cross over with ease.

However, that only went for small groups. The thousand Resistance members could double their ranks, but three thousand dominion troops guarded the pass. It was always hard for a smaller force to attack a defensive point held by a larger one. Even if they had soldiers and strategists with the proficiency to gain some ground, quickly overrunning the position was a pipe dream. Sooner or later, the situation would reach a standstill, and that would give the defenders' reinforcements time to show up and overwhelm them. Shishi knew that, so the news about the additional enemy warriors hadn't shaken him.

If the only thing freaking Jade out had been the additional Resistance members, Shishi likely would have been able to talk him down. However…

©Sacraneco

That Divine Lightning is a problem.

That was an eventuality Shishi hadn't anticipated.

Jade had accused him of being a bumpkin, but Shishi had been in the empire until recently, and he knew of Divine Lightning. It was the Seven Luminaries' ace in the hole. Gustav's Rage Soleil had burned a full fifth of Yamato to the ground, and Divine Lightning boasted more range and superior power—enough to obliterate everything the moment it detonated. "Divine" was indeed the only way to describe its might.

However, after Shishi learned that the Seven Luminaries were helping the Resistance, he'd believed they wouldn't use it.

Divine Lightning had only been used in retaliation for Gustav's use of war magic. By doing so, the Seven Luminaries forced the empire to acknowledge that neither side could use their excessive destructive capabilities without the other retaliating in kind. Coming to Yamato—a self-governing dominion of that same empire—and employing Divine Lightning violated a rule the Seven Luminaries had established. It would throw the whole relationship between the Freyjagard Empire, the Seven Luminaries, and the Republic of Elm into chaos.

Divine Lightning was a trump card, but one that could not be played. The empire wouldn't hesitate to return in kind with war magic. Destruction would devour the continent, and countless lives would be lost.

That horrible possibility could come true very soon.

I had thought them too wise to make a mistake like that.

Shishi had once seen the Seven Luminaries' angels for himself, and the look in their eyes was beautiful. They came across as strong-willed, kind, and sagacious all at once. And because of that, Shishi had assumed they would never act so rashly for short-term gains.

In a sense, he'd *trusted* them.

Shishi had believed that, to the angels, trivial matters like borders and race were unimportant. It was clear to him that their goal was true salvation for as many as possible.

But now...

Did I overestimate them?

...Shishi couldn't shake the feeling that something was off. The notion seeped its way into his heart and refused to yield.

No point worrying about that now.

Fort Steadfast was fast approaching, ever bathed in the moon's glow. The cannon barrel towered above the fort's walls, and the pale light from above threw it into stark contrast, drawing the eye. Just below it, a mass of Resistance forces stood atop the wall with their bows at the ready.

The moment the two armies made contact, and the arrows began flying, Shishi abandoned all hesitation. Jade was right. The situation was what it was, and if he wished to save as many people as possible, he had to end the battle swiftly.

"Follow me! I will clear a path!" Shishi roared.

Then he dashed forward as quickly as he could. He pulled ahead of his men and practically soared toward the fort.

"H-holy shit. He's faster than a horse!"

"The Resistance is so thrown off that they can't aim at him!"

Sure enough, Shishi's sudden acceleration had caused the archers on the wall to lose their aim. All the countless arrows they let loose slammed into the ground and the evacuated camps. Not one of them struck so much as Shishi's shadow. They hurriedly nocked their next round of arrows, but it was no use. Before they had time to fire their second volley, Shishi arrived at the fort's main gate...

"HRAH!"

...and with four consecutive slashes so quick it was as though his hands had vanished, he carved the gate into pieces.

Yet again, it was reduced to so much scrap metal.

One of the lumps came tumbling for his head, but Shishi kicked it away before it made contact, then stormed into the fort. It was a straight shot from the gate to the courtyard where Divine Lightning stood. That was the Resistance's greatest asset. They would surely guard it with everything they had, and there was no doubt in Shishi's mind that the courtyard would be crawling with Resistance soldiers. He was prepared to meet them, though, and charged in, intent on ending this battle swiftly.

"_____"

Upon entering the courtyard, Shishi fell silent.

It wasn't from astonishment at the many foes—quite the opposite. The enclosure was vacant. The only people were the archers atop the walls.

As Shishi stood baffled at the fact the Resistance had left their mighty Divine Lightning completely undefended...

"We meet again, that we do."

...he heard a voice from above.

Shishi looked to the cannon barrel. It was held aloft by ropes and pulleys affixed to the fort's steeples, and sitting atop it was a young woman with her hair tied back.

Shishi knew her. She was the Seven Luminaries angel he'd crossed blades with back in the empire—Aoi Ichijou.

Aoi watched Shishi as she rose slowly. She drew Byakuran's long blade in one fluid motion and descended. Thirty vertical feet separated her and Shishi, yet she landed before the man like it was nothing.

The cannon barrel swayed. Aoi had cut the ropes suspending it. The cylinder, robbed of its support, collapsed upon its incomplete platform...

...and as Aoi hit the ground, the barrel *shattered to pieces*.

Slabs of wood that had been lacquered black with tar flew in all directions.

"———!!!!"

It can't be, Shishi thought. He reexamined the Resistance archers up on the walls. They were dressed impressively in helmets and armor, but he recognized now that the majority of them were women and the elderly.

That was when Shishi finally understood *it was a ploy.*

The Resistance had played a trick, and the dominion army had fallen for it headfirst.

Mayoi was in danger.

"I ask that you not turn your back on me," Aoi stated.

"———"

"It brings me no joy to cut down a fleeing foe."

Upon grasping the actual situation, Shishi had instinctively turned to leave, but Aoi would not permit that.

"My task is to bind you here. I will give no chase to the others, but you alone shall not be leaving."

Without showing so much as a shred of trepidation, she faced the samurai who trounced her once before…

"Come, stay with me awhile. To end on a defeat would stain the good name of Ichijou."

…ready for a rematch.

Shoutou Byakuran, the blade Aoi had borrowed from Shura, was drawn and ready.

"———"

Aoi's talents were such that if Shishi turned away for a moment, his head and his neck would part ways instantly.

Surely this encounter would not be a repeat of the last. Aoi finally had a weapon capable of withstanding her techniques.

Shishi had to fight.

And so…

"STAY OUT OF THE FORTRESS!!!!"

…he shouted an order to his troops with such incredible might that his words might well have reached the moon.

"The fort was a diversion! The Divine Lightning is a fake! It cannot fire! Their forces make for Azuchi! Return to the capital now!"

"What? A diversion?!"

"H-h-hey, take a look at the Amagi Pass!"

"I see torches! There are people going up the mountain!"

"W-we screwed up! Turn back! TURN BAAAAAACK!"

The soldiers caught on quickly once they heard Shishi's roar. A procession of glowing specks had emerged from the woods and was proceeding up the mountain pass.

Unfortunately, recognizing what went awry didn't change the fact that Shishi's troops numbered three thousand. A swift about-face wasn't possible, and because not everyone understood what was going on, the soldiers' ranks quickly descended into chaos. The dominion army had nobody to lead them.

Tantalized by the thought of how much better things would be going if he were back there leading them, Shishi brandished Ounin.

Striking down the angel and returning to Mayoi's side was the only option. Every minute—every *second*—mattered.

The plan Tsukasa devised was simplicity itself. Resistance forces pretended to marshal at Fort Steadfast, while the bulk of their army secretly moved through the surrounding woods. Then, when the enemy troops attacked the garrison, they slipped behind them and marched up the pass.

Including noncombatants, the Resistance was a thousand strong, while the Yamato dominion boasted four thousand ready soldiers, and that was excluding those stationed on the outskirts of the nation. Every Resistance fighter was outnumbered four to one. The fact that their enemy had a man who could match Aoi's tremendous combat prowess made things bleaker still. Between that and the lack of supplies in Yamato crippling Ringo's contribution, the Resistance had no chance of winning a fair fight. In a sense, it was logical that their plan revolved around not engaging.

However, there was a condition if the plan to use Fort Steadfast as a diversion was going to succeed—the enemies of the Resistance needed to view the fort as an immediate, deadly threat. And against an army of four thousand, a mere one thousand was never going to do the trick. As things stood, the dominion army would've been pleased to hold their position atop the Amagi Pass to block the Resistance forces from reaching Azuchi while they waited for their reinforcements to arrive from the rest of Yamato. Retaining Fort Steadfast wasn't enough to make the plan work. Not on its own.

To make up for that, Tsukasa concocted a pair of bluffs.

The first had to do with the size of the Resistance. If it appeared that the organization numbered more than it did, its encampment at Fort Steadfast would seem more threatening in turn. Plus, accomplishing that was very simple. Tsukasa didn't need to hire mercenaries from abroad or ask Elm for help. All it took was sending *the same people in and out of the stronghold.*

By leaving unseen and returning in plain view, Tsukasa could fool the enemy scouts into thinking the Resistance was growing. Back on Earth, the tactic dated back to the *Records of the Three Kingdoms* era, and the Resistance was able to execute the tactic with ease, thanks to Ringo's all-seeing military satellite revealing the locations of the dominion scouts. And as the same people went in and out, the rest of the Resistance slowly moved into the nearby woods.

The dominion scouts became convinced of a growing army at the fort, but the truth was the exact opposite. In the end, the Resistance left behind a mere four hundred people, the vast majority of whom were civilians.

A false show of numbers would only go so far, however. To goad the enemy into a reckless offensive, Tsukasa needed to give another push. That was where the second bluff came in—Divine Lightning.

Divine Lightning was the tool the Seven Luminaries had used to land the decisive blow against Fastidious Duke Gustav and force the Freyjagard Empire to acknowledge the Republic of Elm's independence. Word of its might had spread across the empire, and there was no way that Jade—the man entrusted with all true authority in the Yamato self-governing dominion—was unfamiliar with it. Thus, Tsukasa had instructed Ringo to build a massive fake cannon.

They lacked the materials or equipment to recreate the actual Divine Lightning, but its image had become a symbol of annihilation.

Whenever someone saw a "♡," they associated it with affection or a heart.

Whenever they saw a "♪," they associated it with music or enjoyment.

And when they saw a gigantic cannon, they couldn't help but associate it with unbelievable destructive power.

It would only be a matter of time before Jade connected the dots between that cannon and the Divine Lightning the Seven Luminaries had used. The real Divine Lightning was a missile, yet the people of this world lacked the background and context to comprehend that. And Jade was no exception.

Jade's big weakness was Mayoi. The entire basis for his position was the relationship he'd fostered with the one person who could control Yamato, and he needed to keep her around if he hoped to continue ruling the dominion successfully. If it became apparent that Fort Steadfast housed something that could threaten her safety, he'd be powerless to ignore it. Stopping the danger would be his top priority, and doing so required him to mobilize his entire army. There would be no other options available to him.

The results spoke for themselves. As soon as the dominion army learned of the fake Divine Lightning, it immediately abandoned its fortified defensive position on the pass and launched into a poorly planned attack, discarding its unbeatable position.

After all the calculated moves, Jade had committed a fatal error, enabling Tsukasa to make his move. As the enemy army descended the mountain, the Resistance got to work. Its people raced up that same peak the army attacking Fort Steadfast had occupied and broke through the once impassable defensive position without suffering so much as a scratch.

The Resistance fighters let out astonished whispers as they reached the discarded fortifications at the top of the pass.

"Th-this is incredible…"

"I can't believe it all went so smoothly…"

It wasn't excitement that colored their voices. They were too awed and bewildered for that. A similar sense of incredulity filled Kira's heart as he gazed at the two angels and the elf-eared girl walking at the front of the group. This was the power that had allowed a revolution that began in an impoverished mountain village to end with seizing independence from the Freyjagard Empire.

All that said, though…

"I can see them! There's the Resistance!"

"Stop 'em! Don't let the bastards reach Azuchi!"

* * *

...shouts from behind twisted Kira's expression into a frown. "They're coming for us."

Hibari, the young woman beside him, looked back. "Whoa, I didn't expect them to turn around so fast."

Innumerable torches bobbed after the Resistance, pushing through the darkness.

Their foes were giving chase.

Naturally, the diversion was never going to keep the dominion army fooled for long. Aside from Aoi and the handful of fighters left behind to sell the illusion, the only people left in Fort Steadfast were women, children, and the elderly. They were dressed in armor the Resistance had taken from Fort Steadfast's arsenal, but they were no use in a serious fight. Between that and Shishi's presence among the enemy's ranks, it was no surprise the opposing troops had breached the fort's walls so quickly.

The bluff had fallen apart the moment an enemy soldier breached the wall, and with nothing to keep it there, the dominion army had turned around and given chase.

"Just like we planned, I'm going to take five hundred of our men and storm Azuchi. Kira, Hibari, the rest here is up to you."

As soon as the situation changed, Tsukasa looked back at the pair with his heterochromatic eyes and issued their new orders.

It had always been clear that the enemy would pursue, so before the battle, Tsukasa put together an intercept squad led by Kira and Hibari.

"Leave it to us!" Hibari replied. "Commander Kokubu, keep the angels safe for us."

"Aye, ma'am. I'll protect them with my life."

"Eyeballing it, it looks like the main enemy force that attacked Fort Steadfast totals just shy of three thousand," Kira noted. "I suspect they still have troops in reserve protecting Azuchi. Take care down there."

"Thanks for the warning," Tsukasa answered. "Commander Kokubu, let's go."

The young prime minister cast his gaze over Hibari, Kira, and the hundred-odd Resistance members who would be staying behind to defend the pass, then took the five hundred fighters that made up the main force and began the march down for the capital.

That was where Mayoi, the enemy ringleader and the source of everything wrong with Yamato, was. And that was where they were going to strike her down.

Kira watched the bulk of the Resistance leave.

"His expression never broke. It was resolute to the end."

It was the dead of night, yet Tsukasa had seemed so radiant that Kira found himself squinting all the same.

Kira and Hibari's group was going to stay behind on the pass to prevent the dominion army from giving chase, but the enemy army dwarfed their numbers.

It was an impossible task.

Sure, they could slow the enemy's advance, but they had no chance of actually stopping them.

In a sense, those who'd remained at Fort Steadfast were reasonably safe. Once the attackers realized the stronghold was irrelevant, they would surely abandon it.

Those one hundred Resistance members protecting the route to Azuchi were going to get slaughtered, however. Every person on the pass knew they were being sent to their deaths.

They were sacrificial pawns, and Tsukasa Mikogami understood that full well. How could he not? He was the one who'd devised the tactic.

Yet he hadn't apologized.

Not once did he beg for forgiveness; his expression had remained dignified and commanding even as he left Kira and Hibari's squad behind.

Few were capable of that.

It was an expression of Tsukasa's determination to keep those left behind from regretting their sacrifice. Yet it was also a symbol of his resolve to accept the resentment of those who would die for his plan. Tsukasa accepted full responsibility for his actions.

"He's incredible..."

Like Tsukasa, Kira was a leader, so he felt that keenly. *Could I have done the same thing?* he wondered. *Not a chance.* Were it he, he would have ended up crying and apologizing. As much as that might have seemed like a kindness, it was an act of base cowardice—one that robbed those who were about to die of their right to resent him. The only person Kira would have saved by doing that was himself.

How could he ask forgiveness of soldiers he sent to die? What gave him the right? Nothing, and Tsukasa Mikogami recognized that. He understood, so he said nothing. He refused to permit himself the chance to seek absolution from those he was killing.

"He truly is strict on himself...," Kira muttered.

"You're right. He judges himself more harshly than anyone else and never shows weakness, no matter the situation. That strength reminds me of our imperial family."

"Hibari..."

"That's why I think it'd be pretty shameful of us to take advantage of that strength."

"......!"

Hibari gave Kira a mischievous smile, and when he looked around, he saw that the rest of the Resistance fighters were wearing similar grins.

The sight reminded Kira of what manner of people the citizens of Yamato were.

They hadn't depended on their imperial family's self-sacrificing ways, nor lazed about as generations of rulers put in the hard work.

The Yamato imperial family had a rule: In order to prevent the kind of strife that arose from succession disputes, *the emperor's siblings always took their own lives.* That was how far the family was willing to go to ensure that its subjects lived in peace, and the populace responded to that devotion in kind by offering their selfless loyalty. Each side supported the other, and that unity was the cornerstone behind three centuries of domestic peace.

As such...

"You're absolutely right."

...leaving nothing for their savior but curses as they met death just wasn't their style.

They refused to be so craven.

A debt of the sort they owed to the angels ought to be repaid with gratitude, not contempt.

"Now, let's do whatever we can to make it through this alive. That's the only way to keep him from carrying our nonexistent grudges."

Kira's timid heart swelled, bolstered by the infectious morale...

"The enemy's vanguard is fast approaching! It's the empire's Dragon Knight bombers!"

...and the hour of reckoning arrived.

The first foes to appear were the Dragon Knights, the fastest units in the entire dominion army.

In total, there were ten riders.

"They flew to Azuchi, then went back to Fort Steadfast, and now they've turned around again. I can't deny they've put in an honest day's work," Kira remarked.

"Leave this to me."

While the fearsome enemies cut menacingly across the night sky like a fell wind, Hibari was the first to step forward. She drew an arrow from the quiver on her back...

"Archers, forward!"

...and shouted to her subordinates in the same breath.

Upon hearing her order, everyone in the company with a bow advanced, set their arrows ablaze in their campfires, and drew their bowstrings back, training their eyes on the dark air above.

"Will your arrows reach them?"

"Dragons normally fly well beyond our range."

Hibari answered Kira's question with all her usual quiet modesty...

"But it's a different story when they drop bombs."

...then shot a look into the sky far sharper than her standard demeanor would have suggested she was capable of.

Hibari was right. Under normal circumstances, Dragon Knights soared at too great an altitude for projectiles to reach them. During a bombing run, though, they had to descend significantly for a brief moment to ensure that their payloads struck true. Dragons could only carry a small number of explosives at once, so it was important that they made every bit count.

Under calm skies, they had to drop down to an altitude of about six hundred feet, and in places like the Amagi Pass, where winds were fierce, they had to descend to three hundred.

And at such a close distance to the ground...

"...a Yamato archer can snipe them with ease."

As the words left Hibari's mouth, the fire arrows soared into the night and left burning trails in their wake. Those glowing streaks raced toward the ten diving Dragon Knights as though sucked toward them...

...and massive blasts of flame blossomed in the air.

When the arrows struck the Dragon Knights' explosive, it caused

them to detonate early. Suffice it to say, getting hit by blasts from point-blank range left the Dragon Knights in poor condition. All ten riders and mounts fell from the air, ribbons of smoke behind them as they hurtled lifelessly toward the ground.

"Wh—? Our dragons! How'd the entire bomber squad get shot down?!"

"It's Hibari's archers! The Dragon Knights went in too close!"

"Shut up, you samurai hicks! It's just a handful of sacrificial pawns! We'll overrun them with our numbers!"

The Dragon Knights had gone in first to get the drop on the Resistance troops, and seeing them get shot down sent terror through the dominion forces. However, their Silver Knight field commander forcefully stopped the panic and ordered the army to retake the high ground from the Resistance by charging in.

The mountain slope rumbled as the soldiers surged up like a tsunami.

At a glance, Kira could tell that the enemy vanguard alone outnumbered them by five to one, if not more. Receiving that attack head-on would mean being swept away before ever getting the chance to fight back. And in the face of inevitable obliteration...

"How's your stomach holding up, Master Kira?"

"Never better. I made sure to down all the medicine I had in preparation for this," Kira replied playfully as he stared down at the tidal wave of swords and spears raging its way toward him.

All right, it's time to do as much as we can. Fortunately, we have no shortage of tools to work with!

...he drew his commander's sword and gave the order.

"Squads one and four, release the rockslide!"

On Kira's signal, the Resistance members wrenched free the stakes that held up countless boulders across the mountain pass. With nothing to support them, the rocks tumbled downhill, crushing the cavalrymen that made up the dominion army's advance guard.

"""""AAAAAAAAAAAARGH!!!!""""""

"Damn it! They're using our traps!"

"What the hell?! Now they're in the position we were supposed to be in!"

"Quit charging straight forward, you hicks! You've got room to maneuver, so use it! Remember, you're fighting to save your dominion lord!"

"H-he's right! We have to protect Lady Mayoi!"

"Don't let the rebels get to her!"

The dominion soldiers were dismayed that their own traps were being used against them. However, one little setback wasn't enough to take the wind out of their sails. The Amagi Pass had been carved out of the mountain specifically to serve as a military supply road, and it was wide enough to accommodate a whole army. There was plenty of room to the sides, and the dominion forces spread out.

To their surprise...

"Ahhhh!"

...the soldiers on each edge of the road took a nasty fall.

As soon as they had tried to climb the slope, they crumpled to their knees.

Had the path fallen into disrepair? Was that why they'd tripped? Not quite.

"Th-the ground's slippery! I can't get up the hill!"

"What is this stuff? Oil? Oh, shit...!"

By the time they realized what was about to happen, it was already too late.

"Archers, fire!"

"""""AAAAAAAAAAAAAGH!""""""

The moment Kira brought his blade down, the Resistance's archers loosed burning arrows upon the oil-soaked dominion warriors.

Hellfire exploded across the pass, swallowing it in the blink of an eye and forming a searing wall between the two camps.

Flames engulfed the charging Yamato soldiers…

"Wh-what the hell?! You bastards *know* why they're fighting for their domain lord, don't you?! And now you're coming at them with no restraint? You're some heartless sons of bitches! That's what you people are!"

…and the Resistance's fierce efforts earned a yell from the imperial Silver Knight leading the advance team. Kira heard the indictment… but his heart never wavered.

The Silver Knight's protest was so wrongheaded it wasn't even worth laughing at. The Resistance knew full well that the Yamato soldiers in the dominion army fought only because of the mind control, and that was precisely why the Resistance met them on the battlefield. This was the only answer to the silent cries for freedom from those who'd been robbed of everything.

"Hear me well."

Kira swept his gaze over the enemy ranks and spoke loud and true.

"We stand here today not as the Yamato that was beaten by the Freyjagard. We are a hundred of this nation's best. A hundred who, for three years, never forgot what they were fighting for. Who never gave up in the face of an endless battle. If, knowing that, you still foolishly wish to pass us, then, by all means, come throw away your lives! You can burn our homes, steal our families, and desecrate our land, but you will never extinguish our pride—and you will never crush the will of Yamato!"

""""YEAHHHHHHHHHH!!!!"""""

*   *   *

Their roar shook the mountain far more than a mere hundred people should have been capable of.

"Ee-eep!"

The imperial troops shrank back...

"The will...of Yamato..."

...and the brainwashed Yamato soldiers gazed up through the wall of fire at the Resistance as though entranced.

They could feel an emotion swelling in their hearts, although none of them understood what it was.

Up on the Amagi Pass, the Resistance and dominion forces were finally coming to a head. The dominion advance guard had the superior numbers, but they had left the pass in too much of a hurry to disassemble their defensive fortifications, and Kira's Resistance forces were making full use of them all to stop the enemy in its tracks. The dominion advance guard was in for a rough fight.

Meanwhile, the rest of the dominion forces marched from the empty Fort Steadfast toward the road through the mountains. Jade, their supreme commander, was riding in the middle with the army's central company.

"Shit, shit, shit, shit, shit! You're telling me that Fort Steadfast was bait and the Divine Lightning was a fake?! Are you fucking kidding me?!" he roared, pulling at his hair.

His eyes were bloodshot, and there was no reason or composure to be found in them. The imperial knights he was with kept a safe distance for fear of becoming the object of his fury.

However, Jade found that irritating in and of itself, and he turned to one of the knights and snapped angrily, "I want answers! Why hasn't the advance guard crushed those Resistance numbskulls yet?! They're only a few weaklings, right?!"

Jade seethed with frustration, but he forced his mind to remain on the present situation. His foes had lured the dominion army down to Fort Steadfast, and it stood to reason they would use that opening to try to take Azuchi. It was hard to imagine them having left more than a handful of fighters on the pass, so the dominion advance guard should have routed them by now. Jade had yet to receive any good news from the front lines, however.

Beneath Jade's incensed glare, an imperial knight beside him stammered an answer. "I—I believe it's because they've taken our defensive fortifications and are using them for themselves, and, um... us abandoning our position and attacking Fort Steadfast completely backfired on us..."

"Oh, so what, you're saying it's *my* fault?!"

"P-perish the thought, sir! I'm only stating that because we handed our traps over to the enemy, it's going to take some time to break their line, even with, um, our superior numbers..."

Jade's handsome features twisted further, and he ground his teeth. "What about Shishi, then?! Why isn't that worthless chump back yet?! That damn geezer isn't some chick changing her clothes, so why's he taking as long as one?!"

"At the moment, he's inside Fort Steadfast facing off against the angel dressed like a samurai who single-handedly bested the Azuchi Castle defenses!"

"Aoi...," Jade growled.

"The angel is terrifyingly strong, and she's actually fighting Master Shishi to a standstill! We thought of going in to help, but the battle is so far beyond what we can keep up with, our interference would be a needless sacrifice..."

Jade had seen Aoi's combat prowess with his own two eyes. He had thrown every soldier the castle had at her, yet it hadn't slowed her down. It came as little surprise that she was able to hold her own against the man hailed as the greatest samurai in Yamato.

"Damn it, I'm surrounded by incompetents! I am up to *here* with this shit!"

Were Shishi with the dominion army, his power would have easily broken through the pass. There was nothing Jade could do about that now, though. His frustration mounted, and he kicked the neighboring knight's steed. "If Shishi's not coming, then it's up to you assholes to pick up the slack! Go join those advance guard good-for-nothings! Move it! The only thing you idiots have going for you is your numbers, so use 'em already!"

No sooner had Jade given the order...

"""""————————————???!!!!!"""""

...than a tremor and a terrible roar the likes of which none had heard before shook the entire army as it thundered down the Amagi Pass supply road.

There was something unnatural about the noise. It was like a series of thunderclaps, all ringing out at the exact same time.

Something had happened. The sound made that clear enough.

"Wh-what the hell was that about?!"

Jade immediately raised his head to survey the situation...

"Ahhhhhh! Administrator, u-up there!"

...then looked to where the knight beside him was pointing. There lay their destination: the Amagi Pass's peak, where the dominion advance guard was engaging the Resistance.

The path there, as well as the mountain beneath it, had been reduced to dust and rubble.

"What...the...?"

The sheer scale of the destruction forced the dominion forces to stop in astonishment.

"Messenger! Messenger coming through!"

As Jade sat upon his horse in disbelief, an orderly came dashing from the front of the central company.

"What the hell was that?" Jade demanded. "What the hell just happened?!"

White-faced, the orderly replied, "I have news! The Resistance forces encamped ahead blew up the road and caved in a large chunk of the mountain!"

"WH...WHAAAAAAAT?!"

"We suspect they used the blasting powder we left behind in our hurry to make it to the fort! The advance guard was fighting them at the time of the rupture and was caught in the landslide! Our soldiers have been routed, and they've suffered serious casualties! Furthermore, the supply route has been completely destroyed, and there's no way we can march our army through the pass!"

"_____"

Jade's entire body shook, nearly causing him to tumble off his horse. He was so dizzy it felt as though the world lurched beneath him. Although he remained on his mount, he couldn't stop the cold sweat flowing from his pores.

How...how is this happening?

He'd done *everything right*. Not once had he spurred on his army in frivolity or haste. No, he'd carefully scrutinized all his actions before taking them. Yet even so, his position kept getting worse.

Nothing was going his way, and he didn't understand why.

How had the situation gotten so bad? Jade hadn't made any errors—at least, he didn't believe so. Sure, looking at it in retrospect, the Divine Lightning was a fake, and he'd fallen for the enemy's diversion, but what if it had been real? Allowing the Resistance to keep a weapon that could attack Azuchi directly from Fort Steadfast was ludicrous. His choice to mobilize the army as quickly as possible had been correct. Given the predicament, it had been the only option. There had been no other reasonable choices.

He'd been *placed* in a scenario with no superior alternatives.

"~~~~~~?!"

The moment he arrived at that realization, a shiver ran through Jade's body, and a memory played out in his head.

He recalled the dinner party with the Elm ambassadors in Azuchi, and, more specifically, he remembered those heterochromatic red and blue eyes staring at him from across the table.

Jade prided himself on his diplomacy, and he'd recognized that Tsukasa had been observing him as surely as he'd been watching Tsukasa. However, it still boggled the mind. What enabled Tsukasa to play him so thoroughly? How much practice did a person need observing others to pull off something like that?

Or did Jade have it all wrong?

Was the real reason Tsukasa had read him like a book in only half a day...

...'Cause I'm really just that shallow of a dude?

"A-Administrator, what do we do?!"

"Should we head for the Oono Plains?! We still have a thousand soldiers in Azuchi, and they might well hold out long enough for us to make the detour!"

"We're pushing through..."

"What?"

When Jade gave his order, the imperial knights gawked, certain their ears had deceived them. Upon seeing their expressions... something inside Jade snapped. "All troops, continue on the present course! I don't care if we have to scramble through the rubble and climb up a sheer cliff face. We're getting through that pass and butchering the Resistance down to their last warrior!"

"B-but sir, marching through the debris will make us sitting ducks! It'll be a bloodbath!"

"So what?! How many arrows did the enemy bring? A hundred? Then I guess a hundred of you will just have to eat dirt! A thousand? Then a thousand of you can bite it! We'll still have over a thousand soldiers left, and they'll have the corpses of their useless brethren to pile up and climb over! I have Mayoi's full backing in all acts of dominion leadership, and that means my orders are her orders! Quit your bitching and moaning, and get up there!"

"A-at once, sir!"

As the army stood around flustered, Jade spurred them back into action by glaring at them with the ferocity of a man who might draw his sword and start lashing out at any moment.

There was no plan. He had nothing but numbers and was determined to use them to force through the Amagi Pass.

Fuck this. I'm not going down. Not here, not like this!

Jade's body trembled as if those heterochromatic eyes were staring at him.

Meanwhile…

Deep inside Azuchi Castle, a young woman was gasping in agony atop a futon in the main castle tower's keep. Her tawny brown skin was damp with sweat, and there was a black crystal fused into her stomach. Her chest heaved up and down with pain.

It was Mayoi, dominion lord of the Yamato self-governing dominion.

"Hahh, hahh, hahh…!"

"Try to stay strong, Lady Mayoi," her lady-in-waiting said, concerned. She took a cloth and wiped Mayoi's naked body.

No matter how much the lady-in-waiting cleaned, though, more sweat kept coming.

"Miasma has gotten inside the cut. It was a pretty nasty injury you took."

What she was saying—in this world's parlance—was that Mayoi's pain stemmed from the wound she had suffered when her ear got lopped off. Bacteria had entered the cut and was wreaking havoc on her body.

"Not to worry, though. We were able to treat it quickly, so I'm sure it will heal before long. I must say, though, it was truly savage of them to cut off your ear. And to then join with the Resistance malcontents who refuse to see how just your rule is? They may claim to be angels, but they're devils through and through."

In truth, Jade was the one who'd lopped off Mayoi's ear, but the lady-in-waiting didn't know that, so her burning anger was directed at the Seven Luminaries.

Mayoi looked up at her, still panting in pain. "H-how...is...my darling? Is...there any news?"

The lady-in-waiting gave her a sad look. "Not yet, I'm afraid. I'm sorry, my lady..."

"...Oh."

Mayoi's expression darkened with concern for Jade's well-being out on the war front, and the lady-in-waiting tried gently to cheer her up. "I'm sure that Administrator Jade is doing just fine, though. His force vastly outnumbers the Resistance, and we have Master Shishi on our side. He would never lose to some frail rebellion. The administrator should be back in no time."

It was obvious that Mayoi needed all the energy and willpower she could muster to fight through the disease.

However...

*   *   *

"For now, all you should worry about is your own health...*Lady Kaguya.*"

...the lady-in-waiting's tongue slipped. Her expression froze. "O-oh dear."

"_____"

"Wh-why did I just...?"

Kaguya.

That was the name of Mayoi's sister, and *as far as the people of Yamato were concerned*, it was the name of a traitor jeopardizing Yamato's peace. Why had that woman's name come out of her mouth? And why...why did saying it fill her with such a sense of affection?

A flustered look crossed the lady-in-waiting's face...

"*Why?* Ha. Ha-ha-ha!"

...and upon seeing it, Mayoi burst into scornful laughter.

"That's a stupid question. It's what you people have *always* done."

"Lady...Mayoi? ——?!"

The lady-in-waiting didn't understand what Mayoi was saying. She looked to her ruler and recognized something in the young woman's eyes—hatred. It burned hot enough to spit flames.

Mayoi's rage was so intense, in fact, that glimpsing it brought all the lady-in-waiting's stolen memories back in the span of an instant...

"Burn your mouth with that brazier and never speak again."

"As you wish, my lady."

...but when the stone embedded in Mayoi's stomach flashed, the lady-in-waiting plunged her head into the nearby fire.

Flesh sizzled, and the lady-in-waiting's body convulsed violently. Even so, though, she made no move to raise her head. Her body jolted a few times, then moved no more.

"...It stinks."

Mayoi scrunched up her face as the acrid scent of burnt flesh permeated the room. Using a post for support, she struggled her way up from her futon and tottered unsteadily out of the room.

"Lady Mayoi?! Are you sure you're all right to be up and about already?!"

"Do you need a hand, my lady?"

"Where is it you need to go at this late hour?"

"Shut up. Shut up. Shut up, shut up, shut up, shut up, shut up!"

Mayoi's other servants rushed to her side, and she covered the sides of her head with her hands to silence their voices.

She felt sick and wanted to vomit, but it wasn't because of her illness. It was because of their faces. It was the love and respect in their expressions. Everything about them disgusted Mayoi, and it was because she knew that all of it was a sham.

Under normal circumstances, she would have no value to these people, and they would never...

"Rrrgh~~~~~!"

Thinking about it sent a sharp wave of nausea through Mayoi, and she clamped her hands over her mouth. However, the revulsion refused to subside.

Mayoi felt as though she were going mad.

Looking at their faces?

Hearing their voices?

Having to breathe the same air they breathed?

It was all intolerable.

Jade was the only reason she'd endured it all.

He'd told her to rule Yamato, so she had. Knowing that was what he needed to improve his position, and knowing that she was helping him gave Mayoi the strength to suffer through.

Now, though, Jade was gone. And without him there, Mayoi couldn't stand a single thing about this nation. She wanted to slaughter every last person in it as soon as possible.

That wasn't what Jade wanted, however. It'd only make problems for him. Thus, Mayoi struggled desperately to push down her nausea and loathing.

Please...come back soon... I need you...

Mayoi swallowed her vomit and let tears gush from her eyes instead.

She was in pain and terribly lonely.

The oppressive solitude squeezed at her chest.

She wanted to be nearer to Jade, even if only a little, so she braced herself against the wall and ascended the stairs of a watchtower with a clear view of the Amagi Pass.

Then, as soon as she reached the watchtower's balcony...

Clang! Clang! Clang!

...the piercing cry of an alarm bell sounded from below her on the west side of Azuchi.

"Huh...?"

Mayoi peered down to see what had happened.

The Amagi Pass fed into the city's west side, and from that route came a procession of lit torches bound for Azuchi Castle.

The procession's furious shouts filled the air.

After leaving the rear guard behind on the pass, the High-School-Prodigy-led Resistance forces descended the mountain. On their way down, they ran into the cavalrymen who came from Azuchi when

Jade gave the order to launch an all-out attack, but their foes were just a jumbled-up pile of soldiers with no real formation to speak of. Between that and the fact that the clash was on a slope where being mounted offered few of its usual advantages, the Resistance force was able to pulverize the dominion army with ease.

During the darkest hour of night, the Resistance arrived at the heart of Yamato's corruption—Azuchi, capital of the Yamato self-governing dominion.

"We're here! We made it! After three long years, we're finally back!"

"The enemy stronghold is straight ahead! It's time we take that traitor down!"

"""""HRAAAAAAAAH!!!!"""""

The Resistance fighters flooded into the capital like a dam had burst. There were over five hundred of them, and they were done committing petty acts of domestic terrorism. This attack was nothing short of a bona fide war.

The dominion army gawked in horror at the impossible situation—the *inconceivable* situation—they were in. What the hell was the main dominion army doing? What had happened to the cavalrymen who had just gone to join up with them? Their hearts stirred with fear and questions.

"Stop them, dammit! We can't let the rebels get to Lady Mayoi!"

"Don't fight them head-on! Take advantage of the terrain and cut 'em off!"

It was a small mercy that, like the cavalry who'd gone on ahead of them, these dominion warriors were fully armed in preparation to join up with the majority of the army still off with Jade. The infantry squads in Azuchi quickly drew their swords and fanned out across the castle town to stop the enemy encroachment.

Due to the earlier diversion, the dominion troops were scattered. Their previously overwhelming numbers advantage had evaporated. However, the Azuchi Castle town was still the dominion's home turf.

The defending troops skillfully used the city's lattice-shaped network of roads to launch crippling surprise attacks on the Resistance forces making for the castle.

Or at least, they attempted to.

"I…I-6! H-3! There's an ambush up ahead!"

"Vanguard, ready! Aaand throw!"

"Hyah!"

""""AAAAAAGH!!!!"""""

None of their plans worked out. Whenever they got ready to launch a surprise attack, the Resistance hurled explosives at their hiding spots with disturbing accuracy, ruining the ambushes before they began.

How did the ill-equipped rebels know exactly where the dominion soldiers were hiding when they didn't have a single Dragon Knight on their side? The defenders were at a loss.

They couldn't even begin to comprehend what was really happening. They had no idea that the Resistance—or rather, the High School Prodigies—were looking down on everything occurring in Azuchi from far above the sky where the Dragon Knights soared. Beyond even the atmosphere.

As long as Ringo Oohoshi had her satellite, there was no way they'd fall for any sneak attacks.

While Ringo ran behind Tsukasa and fed him moment-to-moment information on the enemy's moves, Tsukasa took that information and used it to predict what the enemy would do next. "They're coming down Peng Street to cut in front of us and aiming to rush out from R-8 to seal our way off."

"What do we do, Mr. Tsukasa?!"

"We can't afford to let our forces get whittled down here. We're changing course and using Wagtail Street to slip past their flank."

"Yes, sir!"

Tsukasa's tanned, middle-aged samurai attendant Kokubu mobilized the Resistance members. The dominion army had tried to anticipate the invaders' movements, blocking off a road accordingly. However, the Resistance slipped into an alley the next street over and dashed right on past them, practically laughing in the dominion army's face.

"Wh-whaaaat?!"

"C-can they see us or something?!"

"After themmmm! Don't let them get to the castle!"

The dominion forces quickly turned around to give chase.

By the time the Resistance arrived at the main road leading to the palace, the dominion soldiers had all but caught up with them. Although the Resistance's fighters sported only light armaments, noncombatants like Ringo and Lyrule slowed their pace considerably.

Just as it seemed the dominion forces were close enough to grab the Resistance attackers, disaster struck.

"Arrrrrgh!"

"DAMMIT, that hurts!"

Screams erupted from the dominion ranks. Their charge was broken, and the reason for that lay at their feet. Torchlight revealed faintly gleaming metal spikes strewn across the ground.

"Shit, those assholes dropped caltrops behind them!"

"Go around them, and be quick about it!"

Whether they liked it or not, that put a definite damper on the dominion army's pursuit.

Meanwhile, the Resistance forces crossed the moat, finally reaching Azuchi Castle's Nioumon Gate. It was a mighty iron barricade; together, its two doors weighed in at five tons.

When the High School Prodigies escaped Azuchi Castle during their earlier visit, it had taken Aoi's prodigious strength to open the way, and what's more, they were going in this time rather than coming out. Naturally, the gate was barred from within. No amount of effort would be enough for them to pull it open.

Tsukasa had never planned on *opening* the door, though.

"Aim for the support pillars! Aaand throw!"

Kokubu shouted out the order, and the handful of Resistance members at the front of the group hurled explosives at the pillars holding up the Nioumon Gate.

The bombs they used had been custom-made by Ringo Oohoshi. She'd modified the firebombs the Resistance typically employed, altering the way they were packed to bolster their blasting power vastly. On top of that, she'd also reworked their ignition mechanism such that mere impact with a target generated the heat necessary for detonation. This reduced the number of soldiers needed to wield the weapons effectively, making the explosives functional even in situations where blasting powder was impractical.

Any gate, no matter how sturdy, was vulnerable at its hinges. The Nioumon Gate remained shut tight, yet it was helpless before the point-blank bursts. The force from the bombs knocked the gate all the way into the castle, and the Resistance troops trampled over the inert barricade as they hurried into the palace's outermost ring.

"Here's something to remember us by!" a Resistance member shouted.

""""Agh!"""" the pursuing dominion soldiers cried.

The Resistance rear guard had scattered explosives behind them and blown up the bridge crossing the moat.

"Shit, they cut us off!"

"Dammit, those bastards… Head around to the west! We can still get to the castle through the Bentenmon Gate! Hurry!"

With the bridge floating in chunks down in the moat, the dominion soldiers who'd chased the Resistance from the castle town had to delay their pursuit. The Nioumon Gate wasn't the only entrance to the palace. A second access point called the Bentenmon Gate existed specifically for emergencies and also led into the castle's outermost ring. The Resistance hadn't stopped their enemies completely.

However, taking the detour to the west was a time-consuming endeavor. The Resistance had bought themselves a reprieve, and that was enough.

"Hell yeah! We made it all to the way to the outer ring without breaking a sweat!"

"We can do this! They put so many people up on the pass that the castle's defenses have more holes than a strainer! Victory is in sight!"

"Let's keep this up and break through to the middle ring!"

With no hostiles at their backs, the Resistance turned their full might toward seizing control of the outer ring, and in no time at all, it was theirs.

Perhaps owing to how much personnel had been assigned to the Amagi Pass and the rest of the city, the castle's outer ring had no real defense to speak of. There were no archers in its watchtower, nor any guards stationed at its gate, just a handful of fleeing servants.

The plan was proceeding unbelievably well, and morale among the Resistance's ranks was high. However…

"Tsu-Tsukasa…," Ringo called, her voice heavy with concern.

"I know," he replied.

Even without Ringo's satellite watching their enemies' movements, observing the situation at hand was plenty for Tsukasa to realize what was going on.

"Don't get careless!" he shouted. "The enemy is lying in wait!"

"Wh—?!"

"L-look out!"

The Resistance forces had been all gung ho about storming the middle ring, but suddenly, they stopped in their tracks. A storm of arrows and gunfire poured down from the middle ring.

"There they are! I have the insurgents in my sights!"

"Lady Mayoi is just behind us! We have to stop the brigands here, no matter what!"

""""Hraaaaaaah!!!!""""

Atop the stone stairs to the middle ring, a densely packed defensive line of soldiers stood before the Kigishinomon Gate.

When Kokubu saw them, he gasped. "Tch... Th-there's so many of them!"

"They didn't have many fighters, so they decided to abandon the outer ring to make their stand here."

In terms of square footage, the outer ring was nearly twice as big as the middle one, and from the look of things, the enemy couldn't have been working with more than three hundred soldiers. It simply wasn't possible to cover the outer ring with so few, so their decision was logical.

Tsukasa glared up at the Kigishinomon Gate. "Even taking that into account, they have more people left than I anticipated. A fair number must have stayed behind in Azuchi, defying Administrator Jade's orders."

"Ultimately, the one they follow is Princess Mayoi. Ain't no surprise they got cold feet at the prospect of leaving the castle unguarded," Kokubu replied. "What's the plan? There's more of us than them, but they're holed up and have the high ground. And we can't exactly mill about thinking it over..."

"You're right. If we waste too much time, dominion forces will come through the Bentenmon Gate and hit us from behind."

A growing rumble ran through the ground—footsteps of enemy soldiers running from the west. If things didn't change soon, the situation would turn ugly.

That said, Tsukasa had known the situation would be rough from the get-go. Doctrine held that successfully attacking a castle required a force three to ten times that of the defending side. The size of the army on the Amagi Pass had led them to estimate Azuchi held a thousand warriors, meaning that the Resistance's five hundred were far from sufficient.

If anything, the fact that Jade had mobilized the soldiers in Azuchi to take part in his offensive and left the city with so few guards that they'd been forced to abandon the castle's outer ring was already more than the Resistance could have possibly hoped for. Tsukasa hadn't even been counting on it.

No, he'd prepared a different move to ensure that storming the castle succeeded.

"Worry not, Commander Kokubu. Breaking the middle ring won't take us long at all."

Not a moment later, an explosion rocked the air, and lights bloomed in the dark sky.

"Wh-what's going on?!"

"Fireworks? Who the hell would set off fireworks at a time like this?!"

"W-wait, look there! There's someone up on the roof!"

The dominion forces hunkered in the middle ring looked up. A high wall surrounded the middle ring, and a trio of figures stood atop it, silhouetted by the light of the fireworks.

Tsukasa called up to them.

"Hope we didn't keep you waiting, Shinobu."

Hope we didn't keep you waiting.

Upon hearing those words, the scarf-clad girl standing atop

the ramparts—prodigy journalist Shinobu Sarutobi—replied with a cheerful smile that seemed wildly out of place on a battlefield.

"Nope! We just got here ourselves. Just for the record, though, I'm pooped. Going from the empire to Elm, and then hurrying down from there with *everyone in tow* takes a lot out of a girl."

"Tsukasa! Everyone! I missed you guys!"

"Ringo! Please, tail me you didn't get hurt while you were gone!"

The footing up on the roof couldn't possibly have been stable, yet the spiderlike machine with an array of manipulator arms hopped nimbly up and down on it all the same. He, along with a boy wearing a top hat, waved at their friends below.

Ringo's and Lyrule's eyes lit up.

"Bearabbit!"

"Shinobu! Akatsuki! And—"

There was one more person with them, too.

The white-haired girl with wolf ears and a tail standing between Shinobu and Akatsuki was none other than...

"I-it's Shura!" one of the dominion soldiers cried. "That girl next to the ninja, that's Shura the White Wolf General!"

"But that's impossible!" another one yelped. "I thought she was locked up in Elm!"

"Wait, does that mean Princess Kaguya is in Azuchi, too?!"

...Shura the White Wolf General, former Yamato army commander and Samurai General Shishi's daughter.

She was also the mightiest fighter among the Resistance's ranks, and her arrival sent a chill through the soldiers in the middle ring. How was she there when she was supposed to be imprisoned in the Republic of Elm?

As it turned out, the answer was simple: Tsukasa had asked Shinobu to bring her and Kaguya, and she had—*by destroying their*

©Sacraneco

prison. From there, she sneaked them into Azuchi and waited for the battle to start.

Tsukasa had arranged this, and he'd moved the girls into place so they would be ready when the moment came. "As you can see, we're about to charge the middle ring," he said. "Would you mind sowing some chaos for us?"

"You got it!" Shinobu shouted back. "All righty, it's go time. Bear-abbit, Shura, Akatsuki, you guys ready?"

"Pawger that!"

"Mmm."

"Yeah! Let's do this!"

The AI, girl, and boy all replied in turn. Of them all, Akatsuki's response was uncharacteristically enthusiastic. A look of surprise crossed Shinobu's face. "Whoa, Akatsuki. Sounds like someone woke up on the right side of bed today."

"Yeah! And it's all thanks to those special ninja pills you gave me!"

"Ah, right," Shinobu answered. Now, it all made sense.

"They're called 'steelskin pills,' right? You know, the ones you told me made a person's body so hard that not even arrows could pierce it? With those on my side, there's nothing to be afraid of!"

Right before they'd entered the castle, Akatsuki had been moaning about how scared he was, so Shinobu gave him some medicine. And it was the real deal, too, made from a secret recipe passed down through the Sarutobi clan for generations. Shinobu flashed Akatsuki a confident thumbs-up. "Yeah, there *probably* isn't!"

"...Probably?"

"Oh, my family's kept the recipe going for ages, but it always sounded kinda sketchy, so I've never actually used them. I mean, what if they didn't work? I'd be boned!"

"Uh..."

"Just don't go all pincushion on me. If they work, maybe I'll try them out myself."

"Uh…"

At that point, Shura cut in. "Talk if you like, but I'm going on ahead."

"Hey, hey, hey, Shura, hold up!" Shinobu yelped. "I said I'm coming!"

"Don't you worry, Ringo, I'll save you from those barbearians!"

Shura leaped off the wall, unwilling to wait any longer, and Shinobu and Bearabbit followed along after her and engaged the dominion forces in the middle ring.

The only one left behind was Akatsuki, feet frozen and face pale as a sheet.

"Uh………"

The dominion forces in the middle ring had gotten into position to stop the Resistance troops approaching from the outer ring, but when Shinobu, Shura, and Bearabbit got the drop on them from behind, their formation fell apart.

This wasn't just any surprise attack. It was one conducted by a pair of girls with incredible close combat skills and Bearabbit, whom Ringo had equipped with all manner of state-of-the-art weaponry to protect her from the many organizations that coveted her brainpower. The effects were immediate.

Shinobu blinded the soldiers with flash pellets, and Shura followed up by charging in and cutting them down. In the blink of an eye, the entrenched middle ring guards were in shambles.

"Don't let them ruin our position, you idiots!"

"Agh! What the hell is that spider-monster thing?!"

"There's no need to panic! Shishi and that woman samurai are one thing, but without Byakuran or Shiro, throwing ten of you at Shura should be enough to defeat her! Crush her!"

The garrison commander in charge of the units in the middle ring barked frantic orders, hoping to right the course of battle.

Tsukasa wasn't about to permit that, however.

"Garrison Commander, the main Resistance forces are coming up the Tsubaki Steps and heading for the middle ring!"

"What! Why aren't our archers up in the watchtower stopping them from—*what*?!"

The garrison commander looked up just in time to see the pink cloud spreading through the air.

No, it couldn't have been some ordinary quirk of the weather.

"They set up a smoke screen!"

"BWA-HA-HA-HA-HA! Cower in impotence! Your arrows are powerless before the strength of my miracles!"

It was none other than Prince Akatsuki. Soaring in illusionary flight before the watchtower, he blasted out the smoke he used in his shows from beneath his cloak.

"What's up with this wonky-colored fog? I can't see a thing!"

"Dammit, he's farting at us!"

"W-why I never!" Akatsuki cried. "Show some respect, mortal!"

"There's no way you'll be able to hit anyone like this!" the garrison commander shouted up at the archers. "For now, shoot down the flying pip-squeak!"

The soldiers in the watchtower had their orders, and they let their arrows fly. Akatsuki flew left, right, and every which way to evade the volley, yet before long...

"Rrgh!"

...he groaned and froze in midair.

Akatsuki doubled over with an arrow buried in his chest.

"We got him!"

"…Heh-heh. BWA-HA-HA-HA-HA!"

However, the prodigy magician swiftly righted his posture and let out a booming laugh with the arrow still stuck right in his heart.

"Know that I am God Akatsuki! You think your puny weapons can fell a deity?! No arrow may strike me down!"

Impaled as he was, he didn't show the slightest sign of weakness. The pills Shinobu had leveraged to convince Akatsuki to come along had worked.

Okay, no, obviously they hadn't.

In truth, Bearabbit had shot down all the soldiers' arrows with his antiair defense system's machine gun. Not a single one of them had actually reached Akatsuki. And as for the one in his chest, that was a prop Akatsuki had made beforehand by cutting the arrowhead to make it appear as though he'd been struck. The trick was super simple, but combined with Akatsuki's talent for misdirection, the enemy soldiers believed it unquestioningly.

That said…

"As a matter of fact, why not cease shooting me altogether? All you're doing is wasting your arrows!"

Ohhhhh, make it stop, make it stop, make it stop, make it stoppp!!!!

…the ordeal was taking a considerable emotional toll on the illusionist. Akatsuki was a professional, however, so he made sure not to let any of his panic show.

"Instead, allow me to return the favor!"

During the brief opening the watchtower soldiers left while they prepared their next volley, Akatsuki took advantage of the skills he'd honed practicing knife throwing to hurl a green smoke bomb through one of the tower's narrow arrow slits.

As he did…

"Aaagh! This stuff is poisonous!"

…he screamed in a shrill tone much closer to his natural voice.

Akatsuki was copying a trick Masato Sanada had used a while back. Masato was an elite swindler—though he would say *entrepreneur*—and his technique immediately bore fruit for Akatsuki.

""""AHHHHHHHHH!!!!"""""

Akatsuki's fake scream caused panic among the watchtower's archers. They wanted desperately to escape from the ominous-colored vapor, but their station was too cramped for that. Instead of fleeing, they all managed to smash into each other and crumple to the ground in a big heap.

While Akatsuki disabled the watchtower…

""""ARRRRRRRRGH!!!!"""""

…a cacophony of shrieks sounded from the middle ring. The Resistance forces had broken through Kigishinomon Gate.

"Damn it all! Retreat! We need to fall back to the inner castle and regroup! Fall baaaaack!"

The High School Prodigies' surprise attack caught the dominion soldiers entirely off guard. They were helpless, and as panic grew, organizing the scattered warriors while fending off the Rebellion's assault rapidly became impossible. The only person who might have had the leadership skills to turn the situation around was Shishi, and he was absent.

Realizing that his side was facing total annihilation, the garrison commander ordered the surviving units to retreat to the Toranomon Gate to make their stand at the final barricade standing between the invaders and the inner castle.

The dominion soldiers scattered like roaches, but the Resistance had no intention of giving them an opportunity to regroup, immediately giving chase.

Amid the chaos, Shinobu joined up with Tsukasa.

"That was some mighty fine havoc you sowed," Tsukasa praised. "It was a big help."

"Sha-sha. All in a day's work."

"Are you okay, Shinobu? You're not hurt?"

"Oh, don't you worry about me, Lyrule. It would've been one thing if I were all on my own, but Shura was there with me. Besides, all we were there to do was cause a ruckus. As far as fights go, I barely had to stick my neck out at all. If anything, I'm the one who should be asking if you're all right. Are you sure you want to keep tagging along? I know fighting's not your jam."

Tsukasa interrupted Shinobu's concerns by asking her about something else. "Speaking of which, where are Keine and Princess Kaguya?"

"Oh, them? They're hiding in the castle town. Wouldn't want anything to happen to our favorite princess, and besides, most of their work won't start till after the war's over," Shinobu explained. Then, with an unusually serious expression on her face, she asked Tsukasa a question of her own. "Listen…are you really sure about all of this? Joining up with the Resistance out of self-defense was one thing, but having the Seven Luminaries stage a jailbreak for those two is gonna make things *real* awkward between us and Elm."

Tsukasa nodded. "That's not a problem. With their national assembly up and running, there's nothing left for us to do there. Now that they're trying to be self-reliant, our presence will only get in the way. The best thing to do is to give them space; this is the perfect time and way to do it… Honestly, I would've been fine sticking around and helping out a bit more, but it is what it is."

"………"

Tsukasa, as well as Ringo behind him, were both picturing the faces of the imperial exchange students they'd been mentoring. The pair had been wonderful pupils with talent and passion in spades, and there was so much more that Tsukasa and Ringo had wanted to teach them. It was a shame, to be sure, but…

"For now, it's more important that we investigate the global threat known as the evil dragon."

They needed to know if it was safe to trust Neuro, who had tried to conceal the evil dragon's existence from them. Locating the entity who had called them to this world as the Seven Heroes who would oppose the evil dragon was paramount as well. Most critical of all, however, the High School Prodigies wanted to ensure that the friends they'd made here had a safe future ahead of them.

Now that they knew that the teachings of the true Seven Luminaries, the religion that held the answer to all their questions, could be found in the hidden elf village, it was only logical that it should jump to the top of their priority list.

"Whenever you want to make a decision, it's imperative that you understand what you're dealing with first."

"Feels like the finish line's finally in sight, huh?" Shinobu remarked.

Tsukasa nodded. "Once we uncover the truth about the Seven Luminaries' religion, everything regarding the evil dragon and the one who summoned us to oppose it should become clear. To that end, we need to remove the obstacles in our path by resolving the Yamato situation. Let's do this! We have the inner castle in our sights!"

"The Kigishinomon Gate in the middle ring has fallen! The enemy's broken through!"

"The rebel forces are pouring into the middle ring! We can't stop them!"

"Imbeciles, the lot of you! What the hell are our watchtowers doing?!"

"Some weirdo who called himself the god of the Seven Luminaries farted all over them! They can't see a thing!"

"We even tried shooting him down, but he shrugged off our arrows like it was nothing! There's no stopping him!"

"Shit, they're almost here!"

"Dammit! Hold them back! Whatever it takes! What happened to the backup that was supposed to come through the Bentenmon Gate?!"

"It appears they're stuck at the entrance to the middle ring! They can't get through the Kigishinomon Gate!"

"The rebels destroyed it, you idiot! Why's a demolished gate tripping them up?!"

"O-one of the angels who came in with the Resistance mended the damage unbelievably quickly and locked out the Bentenmon Gate troops!"

"WHAT?!"

"One of our samurai who can slice through iron is trying to break it down, but the Azuchi Castle gates are built thick to prevent enemies from cleaving through them. Reports say it'll take some time to get through!"

"A-are you telling me the inner castle is on its own, then?!"

"All we can do for now is establish a defensive perimeter and give Lady Mayoi enough time to escape!"

After their forces in the middle ring were routed handily, the garrison headquarters in the inner castle collapsed into pandemonium. Orders that sounded more like angry bellows flew through the air. They needed to protect Mayoi, no matter the cost.

Then, out of the blue, Mayoi herself rushed down from the main castle tower's keep. Her worry was plain. "What's going on?! Where's my darling? What's happened to him?!"

"Lady Mayoi, it's not safe here! I beseech you, take shelter in the keep!"

Mayoi ignored the samurai's warnings and instead grabbed him by the collar, firing questions with a look of utter desperation. "What

are those pieces of shit doing here?! I need to know about my darling!
Is he okay?! Tell me!"

Upon seeing her expression, the samurai recognized that he
needed to start by calming her fears. "One of our ninjas just brought
back news by crossing the mountains without going through the pass.
The administrator and his company are fine. The enemy lured our
main army away with a diversion, then sneaked around them."

"S-so you're saying my darling is okay?!"

"That's right, ma'am."

"…Oh, thank goodness."

Mayoi was so overcome with relief that she sank to the floor.

The samurai went on. "But because of that, nearly all the enemy
troops are gathered right on our doorstep, and with how they blew up
the Amagi Pass, the main bulk of our army won't be able to help any-
time soon! It won't be long before this very room becomes a battlefield!
Please, Lady Mayoi, you have to be ready to use the keep's tunnels to
flee the castle!"

Upon hearing that, Mayoi immediately changed her expression of
relief to one of panic. "No! We can't let them get to the bell!"

"The…the bell? You mean the big one in the next tower over?"

"Yeah, that one! You have to protect it, or I'm finished! They can't
be allowed in here!"

The bell's power was a secret revealed only to those who would
inherit Yamato's throne. Jade was the one who'd told Mayoi about it,
and her older sister Kaguya likely learned the truth from their father,
Gekkou. Now, the Resistance was coming to destroy it.

Mayoi couldn't let them reach the inner castle.

However, Mayoi's order earned her some reluctance from the
samurai. "I-I'm terribly sorry, my lady, but with the present forces in
the castle, it's going to take everything we have just to keep you alive.
Protecting that giant bell simply isn't—"

"Did I ask for excuses?! I told you to do it, so just—eek!"

Midway through their argument, an explosion sounded from right beside the Toranomon Gate that separated the inner castle from the middle ring. War cries poured in from outside, and metal clashed against metal. The ground rumbled from the weight of so many heavy footsteps. The fighting was at Mayoi's door. Before long, the inner castle would be breached. Mayoi went pale.

What do I do, what do I do, what do I do?!

If things persisted, Azuchi Castle was really going to fall.

She needed to do *something*.

Aha, that's it! I can use the bell to launch offensive magic!

Mayoi had never studied offensive magic, much less used it, but surely with her Administrative Authority, she should be able to use the spirits as an intermediary to cast a wide-area attack spell that would render her enemies—

Agh, no! That won't work!

Halfway through her thought, Mayoi shook her head. Sure, she might well be able to pull it off. Perhaps she could even conjure something on the level of war magic. However, it was still a no-go.

The bell was functionally a magic wand, and the noise it cast all throughout Yamato was how she commanded the spirits. As a result, she couldn't exactly control where her spells manifested. There was no telling what might happen if she used the bell to propagate destructive magic.

Jade was somewhere in Yamato, and Mayoi refused to endanger him. As the princess's thoughts raced, the enemy's voices grew closer and closer.

"Lady Mayoi, the enemy will breach the inner castle any moment now! I beg you, get yourself to safety!"

"Shut up! If I let the bell get smashed, my darling will hate me! I'd rather die than let that happen! Now, quit your griping and go protect the bell! I don't care if you all die defending it, just make sure you—*oh*."

With no forewarning, Mayoi's temper subsided. Her face had been flushed with fear a moment before, but now, her lips were curled into a malignant smile. It was like the corners of her mouth were trying to pierce her cheeks clean through.

"Heh. Your girl Mayoi just thought up a *fantastic* idea."

"Lady Mayoi...?"

Given the predicament, the samurai was baffled at his ruler's abrupt glee. Mayoi's thoughts turned as she swept her gaze over both him and the frightened soldiers rushing around the inner castle.

There were so many of them, yet none were making themselves useful. Each was completely worthless, even after Mayoi had so generously spared their lives. After she'd spent all that time refraining from killing them.

Everything Mayoi did was in service of Jade. The majority of the empire's forces were off conquering, and thanks to her, Jade was able to get the credit for dutifully keeping the unruly Yamato dominion in line.

In other words, if Azuchi were to fall and the bell was destroyed, then Mayoi would no longer have a reason to keep those wretched people alive.

That's right. That's right!

If they weren't useful to her and Jade anymore, then as far as she was concerned...

...they could all perish.

While Mayoi argued with the garrison headquarters personnel, the Resistance vanguard in Azuchi Castle finally pushed forward to the point where the entrance to the inner castle, the Toranomon Gate, was in view.

"There it is! Once we're beyond the Toranomon Gate, we'll be smack-dab in the heart of the castle! I can see the bell from here!"

"We made it! We finally made it!"

Tears welled up in the Resistance members' eyes. The end of their long battle was nearing at last. They had turned their blades on their fellow Yamato countrymen and cut them down, an act as painful as dying themselves.

However, the dominion army still had no idea they were being brainwashed, and they were prepared to fight tooth and nail to repel the Resistance assault.

"Don't let the rebels take one more step toward Lady Mayoi!"

""""HRAAAAAAAH!!!!""""

The charge from the Toranomon Gate began with a great cry and previously unseen fervor. It made sense—the inner castle was right behind these soldiers, and in it sat the keep where Mayoi was.

"At this point, forcing them to fall back won't be an option anymore. They'll come at us like it's life-or-death," Tsukasa remarked. "From here on out, we'll have to push through them by force."

"I know. You angels should get behind the vanguard," Kokubu replied confidently. "Mr. Tsukasa, it's thanks to your plans that we made it to the Toranomon Gate in such good spirits. You've done more than enough for us already. This last push, this one's all us!"

After a great inhale…

"All forces, charge! Pack all your feelings from these past three years into your swords and smash the Toranomon Gate to dust!"

…Kokubu shouted at the top of his lungs.

""""YEAHHHHHHHH!!!!""""

The Resistance answered his order with a fierce battle cry and charged up the stone steps to the inner castle.

For the first time during the entire battle in Azuchi, the dominion army and Resistance forces clashed in earnest. However, the conflict didn't stay even for long. Little by little, the Resistance fighters pushed their way up the stairs, inching ever closer to their goal.

The number of people stationed in the inner castle had been whittled down by deployments to the Amagi Pass and the city. Now it was the Resistance that had the greater army. Still, the dominion forces had the high ground. The question was, why were they being repelled so handily?

It all came down to motivation.

Right now, the Resistance was fighting for every man, woman, and child in the nation. They drew steel to save the very dominion warriors they were clashing with, and they had spent the entire war enduring the pain, fear, and sorrow that came with slaying their comrades. There was no matching resolve like that. Their determination gave them strength and courage, forming a tailwind that pushed the Resistance ever forward.

False loyalty inspired by fabricated truths could never hope to quell a storm like that.

"Shit, we can't hold them! Close the gate! CLOSE THE GAAAATE!"

"Don't let them bolt it shut! Push 'em all the way back through!"

""""AHHHHHHHH!!!!"""""

A mere ten minutes after the all-out push began, the Resistance vanguard broke through the Toranomon Gate and successfully entered the inner castle.

"All right, we made it through!"

However, their victory was short-lived.

For not a moment later, a heavy metallic echo reverberated through the night sky.

*　　*　　*

"Agh! Was that…?"

It was the unmistakable tolling of a bell. Mayoi must have used it to cast a spell. But what kind?

A frown crept across Tsukasa's face…

"Ah…AHHHHH!"

…and Lyrule let out a scream from beside him and dropped to her knees.

"Lyrule, what's wrong?!"

"No, no… That's…that's horrible…!"

"Ly…rule?"

The girl clamped her hands over her long ears so hard she practically squished them flat. Her entire body shook. Realizing that something was very wrong, Ringo hurried over and rubbed Lyrule's back.

However, Lyrule wasn't the only one who reacted to the chime.

"Mr. Tsukasa, the dominion troops are acting weird!" Kokubu shouted in alarm from all the way up the stairs to the inner castle.

The garrisoned troops had changed with the bell's ringing. The moment they heard it, all the terrified panic drained from their faces, replaced with emotionless masks.

"…o……ect……pro……"

"Wh-what's going on? Why'd they freeze up like that?"

"Is it just me, or are they all muttering some—?"

"Protect, protect, protect protect, pro, tect, protect…"

""""Protect protect!"""""

"Eek!"

The vacant-eyed soldiers raised their weapons and charged,

chanting an out-of-sync mantra. The sheer soullessness of their actions sent primal chills down the Resistance fighters' spines.

When Kokubu saw the fear spreading through his army like a plague...

"Don't go falterin' now! The bell's just up yonder! Cut 'em down and keep going!"

...he realized that, as their commander, he needed to set an example before things took an unpleasant turn. If they lost ground here, they'd be swiftly flanked before they got another chance to storm the inner castle. He dived into the fray.

As the man in charge, it was the right thing to do.

"FOR YAMATOOOO!"

Kokubu was no Shishi, but he was a skilled samurai in his own right. Even solo, he was still a force to be reckoned with. He cleaved a path through the dominion soldiers, lopping off three of their heads with a single cut. His rousing display of valor renewed his shell-shocked subordinates' morale.

Or at least, it should have.

"Wha...?"

Instead, they stood petrified by a horrific sight. The beheaded warriors reached out and grabbed Kokubu as they went down.

"I-it can't be! How are they still fighting?!"

Kokubu's expression went stiff with astonishment, but he narrowly managed to wrestle his dominant arm free right as an enemy samurai rushed in to cut him down. He ran his sword through the man's throat, yet it did not stop his opponent, who brought his blade down upon Kokubu.

"Hurgh?!"

""""Protect protect protect protect protect protect protect protect!""""

"ARRRRGH!!!!"

"Commander Kokubu!"

After the first slash, the rest happened in an instant.

Kokubu, along with the enemies grasping at him, got run through by several swords and spears before vanishing beneath the next wave of soldiers.

""""Protect protect protect protect protect protect protect protect!"""""

After trampling over Kokubu, the dominion force surged toward the rest of the Resistance fighters who'd made their way into the inner castle to try to engulf them as well. No one was issuing orders to the mindless warriors. They simply moved forward with the inexorable strength of a tsunami.

The Resistance tried to fight back, of course…

"Wh-what's wrong with these guys?! They're slicing through their own allies!"

"Dammit, I'm cutting and stabbing, but none of it slows them… ARRRGH!"

"Ahh-ahhhh! What the hell's going on?!"

…but there was no stopping the onslaught. No matter how the brave people of the Resistance hacked away, their enemies pressed on, undaunted, for as long as they had enough blood in their bodies to move.

"Protect, protect, protect, Lady, Mayoi, bell, protect…"

"Must, protect, must, protect, if we don't protect, our lives have no value…"

"If we aren't useful, to Lady Mayoi, we die. We die, we die we die, protect, we die…"

All the while, they continued chanting as though possessed.

They knew no pain or fear, and there was no repelling them.

In what seemed like no time at all, the Resistance vanguard in the inner castle got swallowed up by the fell torrent of death, and when

Tsukasa reacted to the disturbance by rushing up to the Toranomon Gate, the hellish scene that greeted him caused the blood to drain from his face.

"Please tell me she didn't—"

"Ha-ha-ha! Haaa-ha-ha-ha-ha!!!!"

Scornful laughter rained down from above.

Tsukasa followed the sound to the castle tower balcony...

"Mayoi...!"

...and saw the Yamato princess resting her elbows on its railing.

Her shoulders shook with delighted chuckles as she beheld the carnage below. "What a bunch of total dummies! Like, I can't even! We've got the idiots who went all nutso after I cast a single little spell, and we've got the morons who came in like a bunch of fools 'cause they seriously believed they could save them by smashing the bell! It's idiots as far as the eye can see!"

"You used the bell," Tsukasa said, his eyes burning with fury.

Mayoi clapped her hands together. "Ding ding ding! You got it, first guess! I used the bell to give them an order. Make yourselves useful, I told them! Protect the bell! And if you fail to protect it, then *drop dead right then and there!* Ha-ha-ha!"

Mayoi's proclamation sent a shocked stir through the Resistance.

"S-she did what...?!"

"W-wait, so if we destroy the bell, then everyone here will die...?"

The Resistance's whole plan had been to save Yamato by destroying the bell, yet their victory condition had been uprooted.

And what's more...

"'Everyone here'? Please, you think I'd stop at just the people *nearby?*"

...they didn't even know how cruel the situation actually was.

From his place in the air, Akatsuki was the first to discover the truth. "Ts-Tsukasa, bad news! There's a whole bunch of people charging through the city, and they're coming this way!"

The thing was, the bell was an artifact with influence over *the whole of Yamato*, and its tolling had already transmitted Mayoi's spell across its full range.

Now everyone whose veins ran thick with Yamato blood had become a puppet and was being pulled to the battle—soldiers and civilians alike.

""""Protect protect protect protect protect protect protect protect!"""""

The people of Azuchi chanted so loudly that the ground shook as they raced toward the castle. Meanwhile, the soldiers who'd come in through the Bentenmon Gate and gotten blocked off by Ringo's newly repaired Kigishinomon Gate leaped into action as well. They began using their own bodies as battering rams and throwing themselves against the sealed iron doors. It was clearly a futile effort, yet they continued again and again. Eventually, the soldiers in the back began smashing into the ones in front of them like a pileup on a highway.

Skulls were crushed between iron and flesh. Gray matter got splattered every which way, and the soldiers squished it underfoot as they continued throwing themselves at the barrier. Eventually, the sheer pressure was enough to snap the bar latching the gate shut. The doors swung open.

With an awful sound, a wave of blood and crushed bits of what used to be human beings washed inside.

Akatsuki had to clamp his hands over his mouth to keep from vomiting at the sight. "Oh... Hrrrrrk..."

"Akatsuki, what's wrong?!" Shinobu shouted up at him.

"The soldiers down below threw themselves at the gate... And now they're all squished and pulpy!"

Akatsuki lacked the vocabulary to describe the grotesque spectacle adequately, but his description was enough for Tsukasa to comprehend the severity of their predicament. He shouted down to the Resistance members who were still in the middle ring, "The enemies are coming at us from behind! Watch your backs!"

Not a moment later, the dominion soldiers who'd broken through the Kigishinomon Gate came charging at the Resistance rear guard.

"Ahhhhh!"

"Dammit! Dammit, dammit, shit! Stay back! NOOOOO!"

"It's no use! I'm stabbing and slashing, but they just keep coming! What do we do?!"

"We fought this whole war because we wanted to save people. We *believed* we could save people. How did it come to this?!"

The Resistance was boxed in, and terror reigned. However, the source of their despair wasn't the deadly pincer formation. It was that their one hope—the belief that destroying the bell would free their loved ones—had been wrenched from them.

That dream was the sole thing that kept the Resistance going, even when they were forced to turn their blades on their neighbors, people who were like family to them. Without it, they couldn't bring themselves to fight the brainwashed soldiers. It didn't matter that their own lives were in danger. Not when these mindless puppets were the same innocents they'd sacrificed three years to rescue.

All across the battlefield, Resistance members got butchered as they lost their will to continue. The people of Yamato cared so much for their peers, and they were murdering each other.

All the while, the culprit behind the grim proceedings laughed from atop her tower. "What'll it be? What's the plan, little angels? If you stick around, they'll eventually squish you flat, but if you smash the bell, they're all gonna die. Think you can do it? You got the guts to smash it? For the record, I'd be a-okay with that. Ha-ha-ha!"

Both her irksome voice and the sneer playing at her lips...

"You would have the NERVE to use your people like that?!"

...sparked the fires of rage within a certain young man whose respect for the *responsibilities of a leader* dwarfed all other concerns.

"Tsu...kasa..."

"Tsukes..."

His friends' eyes went wide. They had all spent a lot of time together, and that enraged roar was unlike anything they'd ever heard from him. His usual quiet composure was nowhere to be found.

"Akatsuki, change of plans! I need you to throw every smoke bomb you have into the inner castle!" Tsukasa shouted to the floating magician.

Akatsuki looked flustered. "What? But if I do that, then everyone'll—"

"Hurry!" Tsukasa urged. "We don't have time to argue. Just trust me and do it!"

"~~~~~~~!"

Tsukasa's instructions brought two things to mind for Akatsuki: the people he'd watched get crushed under one another's weight and the throng of civilians gathering in the castle.

If that many people rushed chaotically into the castle's narrow corridors, the casualties would be innumerable.

"Don't you dare die on me, okay?" Akatsuki cried. "If you do, I'm gonna come haunt you!"

The prodigy magician did as Tsukasa ordered.

All of Akatsuki's remaining smoke bombs went flying into the inner castle. They immediately burst, flooding the area with multi-colored vapor.

Up in the keep, Mayoi cocked her head to the side. "Wait, a smoke screen? But if you do that…"

…wouldn't it obscure the Resistance's vision, too?

As a matter of fact, it did.

"What's going on?! I can't see any—ARRRGH!"

"Dammit, just focus on defense! It's every man for himself!"

"What the hell are the angels thinking?!"

Confused exclamations sounded from every direction as the Resistance fighters found themselves abruptly robbed of their sight. And who could blame them? Mayoi chuckled at the predictable turn of events…

"Ah-ha-ha. Talk about blowing up in your face. What a bunch of dumb— Huh?"

…but her laughter came to an abrupt end.

Suddenly, three people came rushing out of the rainbow-colored smoke that blanketed most of the inner castle: Tsukasa Mikogami, Ringo Oohoshi, and Lyrule.

They had slipped past the dominion forces.

"We…made it!" Ringo cheered.

"And we owe it to you, Ringo," Tsukasa replied. "You never let me down. Now come on. We have to hurry!"

How had they woven their way so accurately around the dominion forces when no one could see?

The answer lay with Ringo Oohoshi.

Ringo could always be found with a pair of goggles hanging from her hat, and they provided her with more than just a heads-up display screen. In particular, they analyzed geological conditions and detected heat sources via thermography. By combining that thermography feature with GPS data, Ringo could easily maneuver around obstacles in zero-visibility conditions. She had led her friends through the enemy line.

The three broke away from the Resistance fighters and dashed for the main castle tower.

Mayoi's composure remained unbroken at this development, however. She had stationed two of the finest samurai in her army at the entrance to the main castle tower. They were no match for Shishi or Aoi, but they were certainly proficient enough to hold their own against someone of Shura's caliber. Tsukasa, Ringo, and Lyrule wouldn't be getting past them.

Plus, even if they did, the keep was designed to protect the emperor. It was packed to the gills with secret tunnels and hidden rooms. Mayoi would have no trouble escaping. No blade would ever reach her.

As it turned out, Mayoi's assumption about her safety was correct. Tsukasa, Ringo, and Lyrule weren't headed for the main castle tower, though.

"What?!"

The group hurried straight past its entrance without so much as a glance. Their true objective lay beyond, deeper within the palace.

They were making for the belfry.

"Where do you think you're going?! Didn't you hear me?! If you break the bell, everyone's going to bite it! Are you guys seriously gonna do it anyway?! You're kidding, right?!"

Mayoi was stunned. Given the situation, the notion that the Resistance might prioritize destroying the bell over capturing her had never crossed her mind.

"Are you actually gonna do it? Your plan is to kill everyone in Yamato?!"

It couldn't be.

Mayoi recalled how Tsukasa had behaved during the dinner party and how he'd denounced her wicked method of governance. Someone that softhearted didn't have the guts to go through with so cruel an option.

"Ah!"

A chill ran down Mayoi's spine. She got the feeling she'd forgotten a critical point about that dinner party, a piece of information more important than anything related to Tsukasa. After she racked her brain, it dawned on her at last.

The three people racing toward the belfry had all been present at the dinner party, and one of them, the blond-haired Lyrule, possessed the same pointed ears of the *highly magically adept* elf tribe that Mayoi did.

"I screwed uuuup!"

"All right, so we know how Mayoi is keeping Yamato under her thumb," Tsukasa remarked. He and the rest of the Elm delegation had only recently arrived at the Resistance hideout. "And by that same token, we know our core strategic objective."

"That's right," Kira replied. "Without the bell's power to compel the native spirits of Yamato, she won't be able to maintain her brainwashing magic. All we have to do is destroy the bell."

"Then the brainwashing will break, and the people of Yamato will get their memories back," Tsukasa concluded.

"Exactly. If we destroy the artifact, we achieve victory."

The way Kira put it, the war they were about to take part in was going to be relatively straightforward. However, Tsukasa had some other thoughts on the matter. "Are you sure about that?"

"What do you mean?"

"The way I see it, that victory condition you've laid out has a gaping hole in it."

Kira gave him a confused look. "A…a hole, you say?"

Tsukasa nodded. "From what you've told us, the bell is older than Yamato itself. I have to imagine that it won't be easy to smash an artifact that's survived through the ages. Or am I wrong? Have you conducted tests and succeeded in cracking it or achieving other quantifiable results?"

"I-I'm afraid we haven't…"

"If we want to storm the castle with a force as small as ours, it'll need to be a surprise attack, which means we'll only be able to carry light equipment that doesn't compromise our mobility. We won't be able to bring anything with any serious destructive punch. If it turns out that our hammers, swords, and grenades aren't powerful enough to damage the bell, it'll put us in a deeply awkward position. Even if our diversion on the Amagi Pass succeeds and we get our main forces into the castle, failure to harm the artifact will lead to us being surrounded and exterminated."

What Tsukasa was thinking of was the Rage Soleil war magic Gustav used to attack Dormundt. Despite Ringo's access to surface-to-air missiles with destructive capabilities that were far beyond any bombs this world had to offer, she still hadn't been able to destroy Rage Soleil before it detonated.

The Prodigies had access to knowledge and technology centuries beyond the cultures of this planet, but magic was the one domain where they came up short. Spells defied logic, and the Prodigies lacked the heuristics to gauge exactly how much of a threat they posed.

Tsukasa knew that without exact information and verified facts, it was too dangerous to go up against magic without at least considering everything that could go wrong. That was why he'd questioned Kira's proposed victory condition.

"N-now that you mention it, you're absolutely right."

Upon hearing Tsukasa's concerns regarding the supernatural traits that magic possessed, Kira reassessed his assumptions as well. All of what he'd told the Prodigies about the bell—how casting a spell on it would spread the magic across all the spirits of Yamato and allow it to affect a huge area for an extended period—were things he'd heard from Kaguya, a member of the imperial family. The thing was, because the imperial family members were the only ones who knew the bell's secret, Kira had blindly trusted Kaguya's words as correct and exhaustive. Now, though, he realized that Tsukasa had a point. If it turned out that physically destroying the bell was impossible, things could turn ugly quickly.

After all, it wasn't as though Kaguya had ever actually tried damaging it.

"In that case, it might be safer for us to go after Lady Mayoi rather than the bell."

"Maybe, but I'd still like to destroy the bell if possible. An object with the power to freely control the minds of an entire nation has no right to exist. I have no problems with the bell's destruction being our primary tactic; I'm only saying that contingencies are never a bad idea. For example…while you're right that restraining Mayoi is one option, another option is available to us. If the bell works like a massive magic wand that can influence all the spirits of Yamato, then I don't see any reason why we couldn't take advantage of that function and make the spirits undo the mind control."

Hibari clapped her hands together. "Ah, I get it. You're saying that we could fight magic with magic."

However, a pained expression crossed Kira's face. "There's just one problem."

"And that is?"

"Aside from Lady Kaguya, there isn't a single person in the Resistance who can use magic."

"Not one?"

"I'm afraid so. Because of how few Yamato people are born with magical aptitude and how many are blessed with tremendous physical prowess, our nation has historically placed a great emphasis on martial skill and offered nothing in the way of magical instruction. Of course...now that I know the bell's secret, I suspect that might have been by design to prevent the artifact from being misused," Kira explained apologetically.

"Then I guess we don't have much choice," Tsukasa replied. He nodded, then turned his gaze *her* way. "Listen, Lyrule, we can destroy the bell, or we can capture Mayoi. But if both of those options become too difficult, there's a third one available to us—and with your ability to communicate with spirits, I want you to serve as the linchpin."

◆◇◆◇◆

"Stop them! Someone, stop them before they get to the belfry!" Mayoi all but shrieked the command.

The people of Yamato were so physically capable that they generally held magic in low esteem. Furthermore, they hadn't interacted much with the elf tribe until just recently, during the last Yamato emperor's reign. There were a lot of reasons why magic played so little a role in the nation's affairs, but now, that very same fact was coming back to haunt Mayoi. The idea that her enemies might have mages among their ranks should have been obvious, but she'd completely overlooked it.

The two samurai guarding the main castle tower, as well as the pair of ninjas lurking in the courtyard thicket, rushed at Tsukasa's group with swords and chain-sickles in hand.

However, the four assailants never reached their targets.

"Ack-chooww!"

"Hyah!"

Before they could, Shinobu and Shura came rushing out of the rainbow smoke as well. They leaped forward, kicking aside the chain-sickle-wielding ninjas in midair. From there, Shinobu raised a *kunai*, and Shura her sword, to block the samurai's attacks.

"Yeesh," Shinobu said. "If you guys are gonna dive in alone, you could at least give me a heads-up first. What if I hadn't backed you up in time?"

"I had full confidence that you would read my play and react accordingly," Tsukasa replied.

"Oh yeah? I mean, you weren't wrong, but still."

"I beg of you," Shura cried. "Save Yamato... Save our people!"

It was difficult to imagine just how much watching Yamato inch closer and closer to the brink must have pained her. Tsukasa and the others did not respond to the grief-stricken plea with words but with their actions. They turned their backs on Shura and Shinobu and continued the sprint to the bell tower.

Then...

"Ack!"

...a stroke from the samurai cut Shinobu's *kunai* in two.

There it was—the Yamato iron-cleaving slash.

"Wowzers," Shinobu quipped bitterly as she looked down at the ruined weapon. Its tempered steel had been sliced through like so much butter. "That's a mean trick. There's no way I'm beating *that*."

Shinobu was no slouch in a fight, but her true calling was intelligence-gathering. Aoi was the true combat master.

"That said, turning tail and running isn't exactly an option, either."

"All you have to do is keep them busy. Do what you can to hold out…"

"You know I will!"

Shinobu was aware of how much the cards were stacked against her, but she stood her ground all the same. Her friends running for the belfry represented hope, and she was going to protect them to the last.

She cast aside her useless *kunai* pieces and drew her illegally modified high-voltage stun gun in its place. Her opponents were puppets who kept on attacking, even with their heads cut off, so she knew the weapon wouldn't be able to stop them. Even so, the muscle convulsions it caused would hopefully slow them down.

Victory might have been off the table, but Shinobu was determined to buy as much time as she could for the others by holding off their pursuers for as long as possible. And it was thanks to Shinobu's aid that Tsukasa, Lyrule, and Ringo made it to the final hundred feet before the belfry.

"No, no, no, no, no…"

They'd be inside within the next ten seconds.

The blood drained from Mayoi's face.

"Stop them! Someone stop them already! Why won't anyone just do what I say?!"

However, no amount of tantrum-throwing would change the fact that none of Mayoi's pawns were in a position to obey her orders. She couldn't catch the trio of Seven Luminaries, and they weren't going to quit.

Despair gathered in Mayoi's heart. Her enemies would ring the bell, and when they did, it would break the spell she'd cast over Yamato. The people were going to remember everything. They would recall the war they fought with the empire and Mayoi's betrayal and mind control.

Mayoi was going to lose it all...

I'm—

...and be *sent back* to what her life was like before Jade rescued her. Her place in the world would die, spelling the return of her old isolated existence.

Mayoi had only one word to say in the face of that notion.

"NOOOOOOOOOOOOOOOOOOOOOO!!!!"

"Lyrule, look out!"

"Wh—?"

The warning came from Akatsuki, still observing the battle from the highest vantage point. While Mayoi screamed from atop her keep, he'd spied her drawing a small flintlock rifle from within her robe.

Before Lyrule had a chance to react, though, Mayoi pulled the trigger...

"_____"

...and the deadly projectile lanced forth.

Tsukasa immediately dived into the line of fire to protect Lyrule, and the bullet struck him squarely in the heart.

Lyrule whirled just in time to see Tsukasa's body crumple from the force of impact...

"TSUKASA!!!!"

"I'm fine!!!!"

...but he shouted down her terrified scream and remained standing.

"My jacket is NIJ compliant. It can shrug off anything up to a nine millimeter FMJ."

Tsukasa drew his own pistol from inside his suit and fired two shots at the castle keep. The first struck Mayoi's rifle and knocked it out of her hand, while the second sank into her thigh. Mayoi collapsed to the balcony floor.

With truly nothing standing in their way...

"Lyrule, you're up!"

...the elf girl hurried onward.

During the battle against Gustav, Lyrule gained the ability to hear spirits' voices. Most mages simply issued them unilateral orders, yet she possessed the rare talent to hold dialogues with them. Thanks to that ability, she understood spirits pretty well. At their heart, spirits were basically like kind, innocent children. They had a much simpler understanding of the world than humans did, so they couldn't communicate anything more complicated than basic emotions, but that was enough for Lyrule to know how gentle they were.

That was the major reason she disliked using magic to harm others. Spirits could affect the world on a microscopic level, and magic impressed a mental image on them, forcing the spirits to use their microscopic powers to change the world on a macroscopic scale. Killing a person with magic was like handing a small child a knife and demanding that they stab someone. If you gave spirits an order like that, they would scream out in grief and terror, but with no way to resist magic, they had to obey. Lyrule could never bring herself to do something so cruel.

Furthermore, Lyrule's understanding of the spirits' gentle natures raised a question. There was something that didn't make sense to her, and she'd been mulling it over since learning of Yamato's secret. Why was it that, in a nation so warped, with its people so oppressed, she had never once heard the spirits screaming?

Lyrule had spent nearly a month in Yamato, and not once had

the spirits seemed agitated to her. Fellow citizens who all loved their nation were being manipulated into killing each other, and she would've thought that being forced to facilitate something like that would cause spirits to cry out. How did the kindly spirits remain so unshaken?

It didn't add up.

Now that she heard how the spirits screamed for compelling the Yamato people to throw away their lives, it all became clear.

It all tied back to what Mayoi had said at the dinner party.

"Who wants a bunch of bummer memories about getting raped and pillaged and having their friends and families die? Remembering that stuff would be, like, a major buzzkill."

The Yamato spirits must have sensed the grain of truth in those words. The nation's peace was false, but they wanted to protect it all the same. In the war three years prior, magic had forced the spirits to participate in the slaughter of Yamato's populace, and although they hadn't had any say in the matter, every choice they'd made since then had been for the sake of those very same people.

It made Lyrule realize how deeply full of kindness Yamato was.

Between the spirits who didn't want the people to be sad and the Resistance fighting to restore everyone's lost feelings, it seemed like just about everyone had enough empathy to endanger themselves on others' behalf—the exact same way a certain village had chosen to take on an entire nation to protect a single orphan girl. And that was precisely why...

...this isn't right.

Those with no qualms about making others suffer to sate their greed were wrong. Lyrule refused to let their selfish ways stand, and if there was a way for her to use her powers to stop them...

...then I'm going to fight!

She was going to do what Tsukasa, the other Prodigies, and Winona and the villagers did for her.

Her powers were unusual, a gift from some mysterious voice, but with only one way to answer the cries she alone could hear...

...then it's up to me to do whatever I can!

"PLEASE WORRRRRRRRRRRK!!!!"

Lyrule ran up the belfry steps and used the great wooden striker like a wand to cast a spell while beating it against the bell at the same time.

The native spirits had watched over Yamato for so long. And now, they were free.

©Sacraneco

The spell traveled from the striker to the bell, where it was amplified before rippling out across the whole of Yamato, along with a deep gonging.

Yamato's native spirits were released from Mayoi's wicked yoke.

The change began with the spirits' microscopic world, then gradually expanded until the effect was visible to the naked eye. The dominion army had been going on a mindless offensive, but now, they began dropping their weapons and stopping their horrible, suicidal advance. The civilians who'd rushed into the castle did the same.

And the spell didn't stop at Azuchi. It wove through forests, crossed mountains, and spread to all of Yamato.

"............Ah..."

West of Azuchi, up on the Amagi Pass, it reached the ears of a group of samurai right as they backed Kira into a corner and raised their swords to strike him down.

The earth spirits that made up their bodies had been manipulated to fill them with a powerful obsession, but that false loyalty faded in the blink of an eye. Their long-sealed memories were free, and they remembered everything.

Recollections of the three years since Yamato lost the war returned, including everything lost, as well as who had taken it and commanded the mind-controlled people's blind devotion.

And they remembered who it was they were fighting.

".........Master... Kira... What...have we...?"

The raised blades slipped from the samurai's hands and clattered to the ground. Tears streaming down the samurai's cheeks stained the abandoned weapons.

When Kira saw the lifeless expressions break, he understood what had happened. The bell's song was one of good fortune, produced by Tsukasa's Azuchi invasion team. At last, Yamato was liberated from Mayoi's spell, and its denizens had their memories and emotions back.

However…Kira couldn't bring himself to celebrate.

"………"

The samurai's abrupt awakening left them overwhelmed, and Kira had no idea how to console them. He and the Resistance had spent the past three years loathing Mayoi and the empire, but the same wasn't true of those under the wicked princess's control. After Yamato's crushing defeat, they'd been robbed of the opportunity to hate the people who'd hijacked their nation, families, and souls. In fact, they'd been forced to revere their enemy and fight to protect her.

All that time and all those lives were forever lost. There were so many things they would never get back, and there was naught to show for it.

And yet…

"!"

…all of a sudden, a dazzling light crested on the horizon, forcing Kira and the others to squint. Kira faced the radiant glow and saw that dawn had finally arrived.

Transfixed by the brilliance, he spoke, "…It's over. It's finally over. The long night has finally ended…"

On hearing that, the Yamato members of the dominion army collapsed to their knees…

"""AHHHHHHHHHHHHHHHHHHH!!!!"""

…and wailed so hard they nearly coughed up blood.

They cried for three years of imprisoned sorrow, for all the rage they could no longer contain, for all the anguish beyond words, and for all else pooled in their souls.

Those wails told Kira that the battle was truly at its end. The tension of the situation had kept him fighting, but now, the fatigue struck him hard. He swayed on his feet, but the moment before he collapsed, Hibari—who was even more injured than Kira—offered him her shoulder.

Her face was covered in lacerations and drenched in blood, but her smile was one of utmost relief. "…We did."

"That's right," Kira replied, nodding slowly. "And now, the true battle begins."

He understood.

The people had woken from their long nightmare, and it was time to start moving again. Yamato would need to confront an unpleasant reality—the Freyjagard Empire would not be pleased with its colony's desire for independence.

Yamato was exhausted, and its people were wounded, but it would have to stand on its own as it once did. Such was the price of reclaiming freedom and dignity.

"I guess there's no rest for the wicked," Hibari remarked.

Kira nodded. "You can say that again."

Come what may, they were going to have to make it work, for this was their home.

CHAPTER 10

⚔ The Liar Knight and the Lonesome Princess ⚜

It was shortly before Lyrule rang the bell at Azuchi Castle. Over in Fort Steadfast on the other side of the Amagi Pass, the duel between prodigy swordswoman Aoi Ichijou and the samurai Shishi was nearing its conclusion.

"Hyah!"

"Hrrgh...!"

It was impossible to say how many hundreds of times their swords had met.

The blades of firefly light and pure-white ore clashed yet again, producing a shower of sparks and causing both combatants to skid backward. Each was the strongest warrior their side had to offer, and they'd spent the past few hours in a stalemate.

However...they weren't evenly matched, and one side was clearly favored over the other.

"Holy cow... That samurai lady is something else..."

"Master Shishi's actually short of breath..."

Mayoi's magic had turned the dominion army into frenzied zealots, and as the few Resistance members left in the fort repelled their attacks, they marveled at the angel.

Shishi's shoulders heaved up and down as he panted. His veritable mane of white hair was matted with perspiration, and in contrast, Aoi had spent their entire bout parrying his attacks without shedding so much as a drop of sweat. And that was *after* having to dispatch a few dozen dominion soldiers who'd rushed in to aid Shishi.

She's strong. Far more so than when we last tried to take each other's heads.

The difference in their skill was obvious, even to onlookers, and it went without saying that Shishi had noticed it as well.

I can't land a hit...

In terms of raw physical strength, Shishi had Aoi solidly beat, but when it came to their respective techniques with the blade, he was hopelessly outclassed. The only thing that had changed since their first bout was that Aoi possessed a weapon capable of withstanding her abilities this time, yet she seemed a whole different person to Shishi.

The samurai glared at the sword in his enemy's grip—Shoutou Byakuran.

Despite Aoi's tremendous show of force...

"...What are you playing at?" Shishi demanded.

"Whatever do you mean?"

"Why hold back? This is far from your full strength."

"Oh? Perhaps you overestimate me."

"You think me fool enough to misjudge a foe after conversing with them through steel?"

Aoi was winning out over Shishi, yet she wasn't even giving the fight her all.

Their battle had gone on for several hours, and Aoi had been given plenty of opportunities to take her opponent's head. She hadn't acted upon any of those chances, however. Shishi was an expert himself, and thus understood that he should have perished multiple times over.

So he felt compelled to inquire why.

With a carefree look, Aoi replied, "My role was solely to keep you occupied until our main force could take Azuchi, that it was. There was never any need for me to slay you. It brings me no joy to take more lives than necessary."

"You claim you can kill me whenever you like?"

"Verily."

"...You would demean me so?"

Shishi gritted his teeth and slashed at Aoi using an overhand stance that took full advantage of his bulky frame. It was an attack designed to slay one's foe by slicing through their head, helmet and all. Thick metal would not have с: ⟨ ⟩ 1 it, y⟨ ' ⟩ ⟨i ⟩ aised Byakuran and caught the strike handily.

"Were I to insult you as you claim, I would not be alone. I am not the only one failing to use my full strength."

"What...?"

"Hyah!"

"Hrrrgh?!"

Aoi lashed out with one of her long legs and caught Shishi squarely in the gut. The shock from the impact caused him to stagger backward, creating space between the two combatants, and this time, it was Aoi's turn to close the gap.

Her pure-white blade arced through the air.

Shishi blocked her strike with his sword, Ounin. As they stood with their weapons locked, each pressing for control, Aoi went on. "I sense hesitation in your blade, and it is not the first time. In our initial duel, and when Shura came to save us and you clashed with her, you never brought your full strength to bear. Had you given it your all, you could have cut down Shura with time enough to chase us down."

"...You mistake me."

"I am no expert when it comes reading into conversations; I shall be the first to admit as much. But I am certainly not fool enough to misjudge an opponent after conversing with them through steel."

Aoi pressed down harder with her sword. The two blades screeched against each other.

"Shishi, m'lord, you are unlike the others swindled by magic. Your will is unsullied, and your actions are your own. Why support Mayoi's system to the point of estranging your daughter? What is it you fight for?!"

There was no finesse to the way Aoi pushed her weapon, merely strength. She was demanding an answer from Shishi, and her intense gaze made it clear that she wouldn't permit him to escape without giving one.

Shishi strengthened his grip on his sword as well…

"I am Yamato's Samurai General. I have a duty to protect its people."

…and pushed back with great determination as he gave his reply.

Aoi was right. Shishi *was* conflicted. He'd turned his blade on his daughter, the people of Yamato, and even Kaguya, the rightful empress. To claim that he carried a clear conscience would be a lie.

However, independence for Yamato was a fool's dream. The war had left the country drained, and it lacked the power to stand on its own. Even if Mayoi was deposed and Kaguya declared Yamato a sovereign territory, it would last only until Emperor Lindworm and his imperial army returned from their expedition in the New World. Yamato would be driven to near ruin again, an ant beneath the elephant's foot.

Shishi wished to never know those horrors again. Living under the empire's heel was the only option that Yamato had.

"False as our peace may be…!"

They were alive, and that was what mattered most.

He was making the right choice.

"I cannot afford to lose here!" Shishi shouted to encourage himself as he poured more strength into Ounin.

The fact that Aoi had locked the two of them into a battle of strength represented an opportunity for him. Aoi's superior swordsmanship gave her an insurmountable edge when both sides had room to leverage the full breadth of their talent, but when this close, technique meant nothing. Here, Shishi's superior strength gave him the advantage.

Now, he could overpower Aoi, force her back, and cleave through her flank during the brief moment he had her off-axis. Shishi had a clear vision of his path to victory and moved to execute it…

"DO NOT HIDE BEHIND SOPHISTRY!!!!"

…but the moment he did, Aoi's enraged thunderclap of a shout rooted him where he stood.

Shishi felt like a misbehaving child who'd just been scolded.

Aoi shoved her frozen opponent back with all her might.

"———?!"

"What could be peaceful about a tyrant who wields ultimate power and forces her people to die when it suits her whims?! You know better than that, that you do! You know of Mayoi's rage! You know the hate she bears for the nation of Yamato! Under her reign, your people are mere prisoners lined up before the chopping block! Their heads may roll merely because she desires it that hour! Surely you cannot call that peace!"

"I…"

Indignation colored Aoi's face as she pressed in on Shishi with word and blade. Each swing of Byakuran was like a bludgeon strike, and soon, every *clang* of steel was accompanied by another, duller noise. Ounin yet glowed with a faint, firefly-like light, but cracks were spidering across its blade.

The battle had gone on so long that Shishi's sword was reaching its limit.

If this goes on…!

His blade was going to break, and with it, his hope of victory.

Shishi panicked, but for all his distress, he had no counterattack or counterargument.

The thing was...

"You know all that and protect Yamato's status quo regardless! What is that, if not a contradiction?!"

...Shishi had already recognized the falsehood Aoi accused him of perpetuating, yet he'd turned his eyes from it all the same.

Now that she was throwing it in his face, though, Shishi's heart was wavering. As he desperately tried to keep his emotions in check, he began plotting a retreat. Knowing that he couldn't fight with a shattered sword, he decided that distancing himself from Aoi was best.

It sounded like a perfectly rational excuse, but an excuse all the same—a reason to flee from Aoi's questions and his own contradictions.

However, Aoi wasn't about to let him off the hook that easily.

"You have a reason, do you not?! A reason you wish to protect this state of Yamato, *even if it means sacrificing its citizens!* But you falter, unsure if that wish is suitable to harbor, unsure if you can justify acting against your position, and that doubt turns you to sophistry to deceive yourself! ENOUGH OF THIS DITHERING!"

"RRGH!"

Aoi had foreseen that Shishi would try to back off. The moment he did, she was already upon him.

Shishi panicked at the abrupt invasion of his personal space and swung Ounin, hoping to block her attack on reflex alone. It was the pathetic strike of a man already broken.

Aoi responded by raising Byakuran aloft...

"What is it you hold in your hand?!
"What do you think it is we swing?!
"A sword is a weapon that steals lives!

"A tool for imposing your will on the world through death!

"It is not to be taken and wielded with a wavering heart!

"To do so is an affront to the sanctity of life, that it is!!!!"

".............!!!!"

...and brought it down.

Her blade brimmed with her rage at Shishi for having lost his resolve as a warrior, and her furious slash caught Ounin on the side, shattering the weapon.

Aoi's attack continued through, cutting deep into Shishi's abdomen.

I...

The wound was grievous, and Shishi dropped to his knees. Then, not a moment later...the sound of a bell echoed over the mountains from Azuchi.

It was the sound of Lyrule's emancipation spell.

Now, all the dominion soldiers still in Fort Steadfast were free from Mayoi's malice. Aoi watched as the people of Yamato wailed in agony over having all their sealed memories and real emotions flood back at once.

"It is decided, that it is."

Her side was victorious.

It was time for their pointless battle to end.

Lyrule's magic freed the citizens of Yamato from the false truth they'd been living in, and when they regained their hatred of the empire, the first thing they did was turn on the imperial soldiers.

The dominion army crumpled in the blink of an eye as the Yamato warriors began hunting down their former imperial comrades.

It went without saying that the army's leader, Jade von Saint-Germain, was also a target of their fury.

"Hey, do you see that bastard administrator?!"

"No, he's not over here! Dammit, where'd he go?!"

Jade had left his imperial underlings behind to cross the Amagi Pass and flee to the safety of the Azuchi side. Newly lucid Yamato samurai were searching for him, their eyes bloodshot with rage.

"Shit, we got careless! I thought he was just some silver spoon rich kid, but that guy's got some legs on him!"

"Don't let him get away! He's got to be around here somewhere! Once we find him, we'll string him up atop a pile of Freyjagard skulls and stick him full of spears so those invaders know exactly how Yamato feels about them!"

""""Yeah!""""

The samurai breathed heavily in anticipation as they spread out across the mountain road to continue their search.

Once they were gone, Jade breathed a sigh of relief from his spot in the bushes.

"Shit! What the hell's going on?! How'd this happen, dammit?!"

As he spat and cursed in a voice that was just about on the verge of tears, Jade made his way through the dense, concealing thicket and resumed his escape.

Everything had changed so abruptly.

The bell's first toll had released the Yamato soldiers from his control, and by the time it rang a second time, the once mind-controlled masses were already at the imperial soldiers' throats.

Jade could barely even make sense of it.

"What happened in Azuchi...and what does that woman think she's doing?!"

It was a bullshit question, and he knew it. Given the situation, it wasn't hard to tell exactly what had happened. However, Jade refused to dignify that *horrible possibility* by speaking it aloud. The only way to protect himself psychologically was to reject reality.

However, that all ended when the bushes and trees thinned out as he reached the cliffside. His view from that height made the situation he'd been trying to ignore impossible to deny.

"No........."

The night sky was starting to brighten, but it was still plenty dark out—enough so that Jade saw Azuchi glowing. Dawn hadn't yet crept above the mountains. No, Azuchi was awash in the light of flame.

Azuchi Castle's main castle tower was ablaze.

"Ahhhhh!"

Mayoi's castle tower was burning.

When Jade saw that, he sank to his knees and screamed.

"Rrrrgh... FUUUUUUUCK!"

He'd lost. There was no mistaking it anymore.

His foes had taken Azuchi, and the spell Mayoi had cast over Yamato was broken. Mayoi was very likely dead...and even if she'd survived, she certainly wasn't in any state to ring the bell again.

The jaws of defeat had well and truly clamped shut. There was no victory to be salvaged from them.

All Jade's successes from the past several years had evaporated as though they'd never existed at all.

Jade began tearing at his hair...

"Shit! Where'd that little bastard disappear to?! Just give it up and show yourself already!"

"Eep!"

...but when he heard his pursuers angrily shouting as they searched through the brush behind him, his entire body shook.

F-first things first—I gotta get out of here...

After Mayoi's magic got lifted and the Yamato samurai returned to their senses, the remaining Freyjagard forces met a grisly fate. The samurai were so profoundly enraged at being dominated and having their nation destroyed by the very person who sold them out that they gouged out the eyes and cut off the noses and ears of any imperials they came across before beheading them.

Jade shuddered in fear as he recalled the agonized screams of his soldiers while they were hacked to pieces.

He had no desire to go out like that. It was no decent way for any human being to die. Escape was Jade's only option.

He needed a chance to slip away.

A thought crossed his mind, and upon looking over the cliff edge to see how far of a drop it was...

"I-is that what I think it is?!"

...his eyes gleamed.

Jade had spotted something at the bottom of the thirty-foot-tall cliff: a horse. It had been fitted with a Freyjagardian saddle, and it munched idly on some grass.

Originally, the steed had belonged to one of the imperial soldiers who'd obeyed Jade's rash order to come up the pass from Azuchi but had gotten struck down by Tsukasa and the main Resistance forces on their way there.

That horse was salvation in Jade's hour of need, a gift from the heavens, sent to deliver him from despair.

With the dexterity he'd cultivated in his youth, Jade was able to climb down without issue, and the horse was his. He wasted no time mounting the beast and taking its reins. It was a fine, well-trained steed, and with its help, he would finally be able to shake those Yamato samurai.

Luckily for Jade, he'd pulled in Yamato soldiers from all across the nation to stamp out the Resistance, and all of them were still concentrated in or around Azuchi. The road checkpoints were practically unmanned, and border security was paltry. Finding an opening and slipping through it would be child's play.

Jade was going to make it. He was going to get away.

Yamato samurai wouldn't chase him beyond the Freyjagard Empire's border.

All he had to do was cross it.

"You'd do well to remember who it is that's letting you live in this house, kid."

All he had to do was go back...

"Say, little mongrel, don't you think Charlotte's earrings would look so much better on me? Run on over to her mansion and snag them for me."

Back to the empire...

"Hey, Jade, what's the big idea, scoring better than me on that test?! You've got a lot of nerve for a filthy whoreson! You're gonna pay for this, big time!"

"...I'm such an idiot," Jade mumbled self-derisively. "I can go back...but there's nothing for me there..."

As images from his past flickered through his mind, Jade hung his head. Fleeing to the empire would leave him nothing but his life.

No one waited to help him. He had no family that would offer shelter.

I've always had nothing. That's the whole damn reason I tried to get my hands on everything.

It all happened in a flash.

As soon as Lyrule's spell freed the Yamato members of the dominion army, wails of rage erupted from all over. Their anger spread to the Resistance as well, and it wasn't long before all semblance of order broke down, and they became an enraged mob. Carried by their wrath, they stampeded toward the castle tower where the enemy ringleader, Mayoi, was holed up.

Once they had the tower surrounded, they set it alight.

With the proper battle over, the act was nothing more than vigilante justice. Naturally, Tsukasa had some objections.

However, the people of Yamato were in no mood to hear him out…

"Tsu…kasa…"

"Everything's going to be okay, Ringo. Just stay behind me."

…and a group of Yamato samurai had encircled him and the rest of the delegation from Elm with their weapons drawn.

As Ringo and Lyrule cowered in fear, Tsukasa stepped in front of them and glared at the samurai with his heterochromatic eyes.

"I can't say I much appreciate being treated this way. We've been nothing but friendly to you all, and we played a sizable role in your retaking the country. The way I see it, you have no justification whatsoever for turning your swords on us."

One of the samurai gave him a deep nod. "You're absolutely right. And as such, if any of us should so much as graze your skin with our steel, the guilty party will sever their own head on the spot."

"What?!"

"We owe you a great debt, and if we were to do you harm, we would have no way to atone but with our lives. Admittedly, we would rather things never come to that. So please, turn a blind eye here. We have no desire to attack you."

"_____"

The look in the samurai's eyes was dead serious.

If Tsukasa tried to push through by force and ended up letting their blades so much as nick him, they had every intention of slashing their own throats to atone for repaying the Prodigies' goodwill with violence.

"Shura…"

"…Forgive me, Shinobu. But the younger princess took everything from us, and we cannot allow her to live. Until her head rolls,

our war will never end, and we can't prepare for the next fight while amid this one. This is the way things are..."

"How dare you sell out our nation!"

"Die! Pay for your sins with your life, you turncoat!"

"You disgrace every member of the imperial family who died so that Yamato could prosper!"

"Your ancestors would be ashamed of you! Traitor! Murderer!"

The people shouted and jeered at the treasonist princess who trampled on their dignity and betrayed their nation, and as though in response to their rage, the fire grew in intensity and swallowed the tower's entire base.

Unfortunately for Mayoi, her leg was still wounded from Tsukasa's gunshot. She had no way to escape.

Realizing that he'd become complicit in an extrajudicial execution, Tsukasa glowered.

"Worry not," Shura told him. "She was already scheduled to be executed, *even before our war with Freyjagard.*"

"What are you talking about?"

"Three years ago, just before the war, three of the maids working at her residence disappeared. At first, it was treated as a missing person case, but her older sister had just taken the throne at the time, and when she ordered the Imperial Household Ministry's Special Forces to inspect the younger princess's residence, they found three corpses in the basement that had been tortured to death."

"And you're saying...that Mayoi was the culprit?"

Shura nodded. "The Special Forces became certain of that after their investigation, and after the younger princess was apprehended, the older princess sentenced her to death by sawing. A member of the imperial family had committed the grave sin of murder, and in accordance with Yamato's laws, it was Kaguya's duty to carry out the execution herself."

"…Why would Mayoi do something like that?"

"I don't know, and I don't care," Shura replied. "I have no interest in the motives of a woman who would betray her nation to save herself." Her voice dripped with vitriol as she stared up in disgust at the tower keep. The flames climbed ever higher.

"What's the plan? If Bearabbit and I work together, I'm pretty sure we could force our way through and save little miss princess," Shinobu asked Tsukasa, signaling him with Morse code so as not to let Shura understand.

"No, sit tight. That would be a dangerous move, even for you. Not to mention we've got Ringo's and Lyrule's safety to consider." Tsukasa believed this was no time to be making risky plays. *"I can't say that this vigilante justice sits well with me, but Mayoi's crimes certainly warrant action, and it is true that she needs to take responsibility for what she's done. We need to prioritize our own safety here. For now, just hold your position and don't do anything."*

"Roger that."

After telling Shinobu to back down, Tsukasa took another look at the tower. Its second floor was already burning.

Then a thought crossed his mind.

Something didn't add up.

According to Shura, Mayoi committed some murders before the war broke out. From Tsukasa's perspective, though, that information didn't sit right. It didn't quite match what he'd seen of Mayoi's hatred. Mayoi *loathed* Yamato, enough that she seemed likely to butcher its entire populace at any moment. Her supposed actions didn't align with the image Tsukasa had of her.

There's no way her hatred would ever have been sated by killing a mere three people…

"It is decided, that it is."

"_____"

The wound on Shishi's flank was deep, and it brought him to his knees.

His large wolf ears caught voices from all around. The people of Yamato were themselves again, and their sorrowful wails filled the air. They mourned for what they had lost and cursed the years they'd spent bowing to a usurper.

Those cries were proof of just how much they had loved the old regime.

Shishi had claimed that he wanted to protect the fabricated status quo for their sake, but that had all been a sham. To them, a false peace was worthless.

Aoi watched the freed people for a moment, then turned to Shishi. "It is something to be proud of, that it is. It takes a fine nation to inspire its people to protect it so, even to the point of abandoning peace. And it takes a fine hand to build a land so beloved by those who call it home. Winning back your independence may be arduous, but when the people call for it, a warrior must risk their life to give it to them."

Shishi nodded solemnly. "...You speak true. I know. I have always known what a fine, virtuous nation Yamato is."

Its people had the power to do anything they set their minds to. Yet for all the might they possessed, they never let it go to their heads. Quite the contrary, in fact. They were fully aware of the responsibility that great strength carried, and they were always their own harshest judges.

For generations, the Yamato imperial family had embodied that sense of virtue. That was why the citizens loved and respected their homeland so deeply, and it was why the imperial family inspired such unflinching loyalty that people were willing to sacrifice their lives for them.

Shishi didn't need Aoi to tell him any of that. None had served Yamato longer or more faithfully than he had.

He knew the truth better than anyone.

"And so, too, do I know that the uncompromising Yamato virtues..."

"No! I don't want to die! Please, save me! I want to liiiive!"

"...cast a little girl into the darkest depths of hell!"

An echo of that fateful day conjured new strength, and Shishi struggled to his feet.

"Take care not to strain yourself. Moving around with a wound like that will surely be the death of you," Aoi warned as she saw blood gush from the man's side.

However, Shishi paid her no heed...

"Do you know how the imperial family has maintained the peace for so many generations, Angel Aoi? They possess the kind of state power that breeds greed and bitterness, yet they never became a privileged class like the Freyjagard nobles, and they are revered and supported by all. Can you imagine how that *impossible miracle* came to be?!"

...and shouted while reaching for his *wakizashi* short sword.

"The answer is simple. Out of all the people in Yamato, *the members of the imperial family make more personal sacrifices than anyone else to bring peace to our land and to those who live in it.* Why, they even built a convenient performance to show off how self-sacrificing they were right into their administrative system. And Lady Mayoi was a *tool* to serve that end!"

As Shishi made his indictment, his thoughts turned. He considered the nation of Yamato and his life living in it.

During his childhood, his parents and their contemporaries told him stories about how great the Yamato imperial family was.

As he grew, he once witnessed that virtue with his own eyes and decided to hone his swordsmanship to better serve his home.

His efforts eventually paid off, and he was appointed Samurai General, and on that same day, he learned the shocking truth.

Yamato's Samurai General oversaw the management of all the nation's soldiers, and when Shishi promoted him, he had no choice but to learn about the other side of Yamato: the twisted things its imperial family engaged in to maintain the impossible miracle.

"Whenever a new ruler is crowned in Yamato, it is the custom that their siblings commit seppuku to ensure there can never be a conflict for the throne. It's an extreme practice, but the imperial family has adhered to it for generations without so much as a complaint. Their willing sacrifice for the sake of peace inspires great reverence from the citizens."

To the people of Yamato, that was their model of how virtuous adults should comport themselves.

"But the truth behind that ritual…was far different than what we imagined."

It was difficult for any rationally thinking individual to trust that a single family had consistently produced offspring willing to kill themselves for centuries.

Unsurprisingly, there was a trick to it.

The truth was that younger siblings were born and raised *for the sole purpose of dying on schedule.* Their residences were shut off from everything, and they were afforded none of the world's joys or wonders. They were barely treated as human. Instead, they became tools reared only to put on a show of dying without hesitation.

Nevertheless, learning that did nothing to shake Shishi's loyalty. After all, it was an undeniable truth that the imperial family's willingness to shed its own blood was what had bought the nation such a prolonged time of peace.

Yamato emperors had sacrificed the good of the few in exchange for that of the many. If you looked at the way the Freyjagard Empire oppressed its citizens to benefit a small handful of nobles, the people of Yamato were incomparably well off.

As Samurai General, Shishi chose to endorse the system. Now that he had the whole truth, he still felt that the citizenry's well-being should come first. As a samurai, he was proud of his responsibility. His was a fine and virtuous duty.

It wasn't until the day he saw Mayoi sobbing and pounding on her prison cell that his pride turned to self-loathing.

Upon hearing her heartbroken screams, everything changed for him.

Mayoi had been sentenced to death after getting charged with murdering her maids, but she banged incessantly on her cell and professed her innocence. And she had every right to, for she hadn't harmed anyone. The alleged murders had never taken place.

The whole incident was a lie cooked up by Kaguya and the Imperial Household Ministry's Special Forces. Mayoi had *refused to commit suicide*, but putting her to death allowed the dog and pony show demonstrating Kaguya's virtue to continue.

"*Please, save me... I finally...found a reason to live... Meeting Jade...was the first time I ever enjoyed living...but now... No, no... I don't want to die... Shishi, please, save me... I won't try to usurp the throne, I promise... I don't want to be empress...and I'll never defy my sister... So please, don't let them kill me...*"

Mayoi's cries still rang in his ears.

Her voice was hoarse from screaming the whole night through, yet still, she begged for his aid.

And with Shishi knowing everything, how had he responded?

How did he answer her plea?

"*Lady Mayoi, as Lady Kaguya's younger sister, your suicide is of great importance. Your death will not be in vain. You will become the earth on which Yamato is built, and your memory will live on and be revered both in history and in the people's hearts. I beseech you, it is not too late to choose an honorable death. If you do, I will put my life on the line to convince Lady Kaguya and the Special Forces to allow you to go through with it—"*

"You utter REPROBATE!!!!"

Shishi was no longer able to contain himself, and his rage came out as a murderous roar. If he could have struck his past self down, he would have done so without hesitation.

"I was an adult telling a child to kill herself! What virtue was there in that?!"

Something had been seriously wrong with him.

How could he have believed that was righteous? What deception did he feed himself to think it was just?

Perhaps, where the general public was concerned, sacrificing the good of the few in exchange for the good of the many was the honorable thing to do.

Yet Shishi could not abide it any longer.

He was sick and tired of any ideal that would have him refuse to save those suffering injustice before his very eyes.

"Thanks to you, I see clearly now. I know what lies I told myself, what I told myself in earnest, what I stayed in this country to protect!"

It was clear to him now who needed him.

"She asked me to save her, and no respectable adult would ever refuse a child's plea."

It was time for him to go to her and fulfill his long-neglected duties!

"I will see this through, no matter what it takes! To ensure I never stray from the proper path again!!!!"

*   *   *

The fires of passion burned in Shishi's eyes as he unsheathed his *wakizashi*.

He was casting aside his virtue as the Samurai General, his loyalty to Yamato, his duty, and everything else he had—all so he could save a single girl.

Shoutou Ounin lay broken, and his *wakizashi* was an undoubtedly lesser blade. It stood no chance against Byakuran. This would hardly be a fight, even ignoring Shishi's wound. Blood still flowed from it, and Shishi likely had only a few hours left.

Still, he didn't hesitate.

He strode forward.

"——?!"

Shishi had been ready to do or die, but he stopped abruptly in his tracks.

And why?

Because Aoi had thrust Byakuran into the ground at his feet.

As the man's eyes went wide in surprise and confusion…

"Were it I, I would be ill at ease heading to so crucial a battle with so meager a blade."

…Aoi spoke.

"Shoutou Byakuran can take no more, not after our clash. In my hands, even a single swing would be too much for it to bear. However…she is a gentle blade, that she is. Were she to aid a friend of her homeland, to carry out what her wielder believed was right, she would deliver a most glorious final slash."

And with that…

"Fare thee well, Shishi, m'lord."

…Aoi smiled merrily.

Shishi found her actions befuddling, but that grin made everything clear.

©Sacraneco

Now he realized that *this was the way Aoi had been fighting her whole life*. There was no shortage of noble causes offering reasons not to save people, but she spared them no attention and lent them no ear. Whenever the world's injustices caused the weak to shed tears, she was always there fighting for them.

Even if she knew it would make a thousand enemies close at hand and ten thousand more beyond the horizon, she drew her sword all the same.

Not once had Aoi ever given in to self-deception, and now that Shishi had chosen to walk the same path, she was giving him the strength to see it through.

She has bested me, well and truly...

After losing his way so completely, Shishi finally stood eye to eye with the samurai before him.

And so...

"I am in your debt."

...Shishi thanked her as he pulled Byakuran, cracks and all, from the earth.

The moment he did, a silver wind sped over Fort Steadfast's tall ramparts and swooped down beside them.

That wind...

"Sh-Shiro!"

...was none other than the silvery-white wolf who had led Aoi and the rest of the Elm delegation to the Resistance hideout.

Upon landing next to Shishi and Aoi, Shiro turned to the heavens and howled.

Awooooooo...

His cry soared, as though to reach the fading moon.

When he did, the obsidian crystal fused into his back flashed, causing rays of light to travel along Shiro's body like blood vessels. Then he began visibly transforming. His body more than doubled in size, his claws grew longer and sharper, and the obsidian crystal spread until it reached about halfway down his legs.

"I-is this...the same as what happened to the Lord of the Woods and the Fastidious Duke?!" Aoi stood aghast.

"............."

Shiro paid her astonished gawking no heed. Once his transformation was complete, he stared silently at the *byuma* samurai.

Shishi could tell what the wolf was saying.

"You will allow me to ride you once more, then?"

Awoo!

Shishi was overcome with gratitude at how dutifully Yamato's guardian deity had watched over him and his daughter. "I apologize for all the worry I caused you. I should be old enough to know better, but all I've done is lose my way... I may not have much life left in me, but I feel as though I finally know who I am. And so...I intend to use my remaining time to hold true to myself."

"____"

Shiro lay prostrate as his way of telling Shishi to hurry.

With Byakuran in hand, the dying samurai mounted the great wolf's back, bleeding all over the beast's beautiful coat.

"Now please, lend me your aid!"

AWOOOOOOOOOOO!!!!

With a great howl, Shiro soared into the air like the wind.

He had no need for a running start. With a single bound, the wolf cleared the fortress walls and began making his way toward the Amagi Pass.

"M-Ms. Aoi!"

Resistance soldiers came rushing over in a panic.

"A-are you sure it's all right to let Master Shishi get away?! Unlike everyone else, he served Princess Mayoi of his own free will! If he gets to Azuchi, our main forces could be in danger!"

"Worry not."

Aoi didn't share their concerns.

"Immediate treatment may have saved him, but with how much he is moving, that wound will surely be fatal. My comrades will not lose to a dying man whose sword barely has a single swing left. The most he can do now…is save but one fading life from the ruins of this fruitless war."

Aoi looked in the direction Shiro had gone.

Her gaze was tinged with anxiety, but only slightly. Shishi was likely beyond the pass by now, and though she knew she would never see him again, she prayed that in his final moments, he would be able to carry out his will successfully.

"Sellout! Traitor!"

"Apologize to all the past emperors' siblings by dying, you shameless coward!"

"Thousands of people perished because of you! Burn in hell!"

"Give us back our lives! Give us back our country!"

The fires of rage devouring Azuchi Castle's inner castle had finally risen up the whole length of the castle tower.

Mayoi had fled, dragging her immobile, gunshot-wounded leg behind her, but she was at the top floor now, and there was nowhere left to run.

"Ah! It burns!"

She screamed and reeled back as the flames licked at her toes.

"Hahhh, hahhh... Khhff! Khoff!"

Even breathing hurt. With every breath, scalding air seared her lungs, preventing her from taking a decent inhale. On top of that, she was still fighting through an infection, and her ear and leg were both injured.

There was only so much her body could endure.

Mayoi sank to the floor and leaned against a pillar, unable to take another step.

""""Give them back! Give them back!! Give them back!!!!""""

Meanwhile, the jeering and booing continued raining down on her like thunder.

There was so much rage in their voices, and they echoed so strongly that the castle tower practically shook. Mayoi gritted her teeth.

"What...? What the hell...?"

Mayoi dug her fingers into the floor, snapping her long nails, but she didn't care. She was so mad.

That she had taken much from Yamato was undeniable. She had robbed its people of their history, pride, land, and their very lives. She knew all that.

But at the same time...what gave them the right to condemn her so harshly?

"You people stole everything from me, too, you know!!!!"

Mayoi's furious rebuttal spilled out of her smoke-clogged throat like a sob, and perhaps it truly was. At the same time, her impending death caused her life—her needlessly long, empty existence—to flash before her eyes.

When a new emperor took the throne in Yamato, it was customary for all their siblings to commit suicide. This not only prevented power struggles from breaking out and destabilizing the nation, but it also allowed the imperial family to visibly demonstrate to the uneducated populace the lengths they'd go to for national peace.

It took ages to cultivate, but by closing off their country so as to keep the influence of foreign culture to a minimum, devising a self-execution method called *seppuku* that was exclusive to their nation, manufacturing the concept of an honorable death, and fostering the idea that sacrificing your life for others was something to be proud of...

...Yamato's rulers had established a method that effectively gave them a stranglehold on the will of the people.

Unsurprisingly, the two sisters Kaguya and Mayoi fell prey to this system the moment they were born. As the older sister, Kaguya was raised in Azuchi Castle so she could become Yamato's next empress. As the younger one, Mayoi was locked away in a residence on the city's outskirts to mold her into a tool who would willingly end her own life and demonstrate the imperial family's devotion on the day of Kaguya's ascension.

The second child's role didn't stop there, however. If anything were to happen to the true heir apparent, it was Mayoi's job as a "spare" to become Kaguya and take the throne in her place. In her isolated home, she was robbed of all freedom and raised solely to carry out that task.

She wore the same clothes as Kaguya.

She had the same hairstyle as Kaguya.

She took the same lessons as Kaguya.

She ate the same foods as Kaguya.

Nothing else was permitted. She was denied all agency.

She wasn't allowed to read books Kaguya hadn't read.

She wasn't allowed to eat foods Kaguya hadn't eaten.

She merely imitated Kaguya's life with mechanical precision, never once afforded any autonomy.

If Kaguya got injured, they hurt her in the same spot.

If Kaguya got a mole, they used a heated drill to give her one, too.

Mayoi's entire life revolved around becoming the best replacement for Kaguya she could be. There was only one thing that differentiated her, and it was that she never received any of the love her elder sister did.

Everyone Mayoi interacted with at the residence was part of the Special Forces, from those who dressed her to her instructors to her guards, and not a single one of them treated her like a person.

Thinking back now, Mayoi realized that was part of the Yamato imperial family's system as well. She was a tool designed to die, so they didn't want her to get attached to living. They had spent generations polishing and perfecting their methods for raising obedient sacrificial lambs, and their methods worked like a charm. Fish who lived in the lightless ocean depths didn't need eyes, so they eventually stopped growing them altogether, and in much the same way, Mayoi's constant suppression wore away at her ability to feel. Eventually, all her emotions atrophied away.

Over time, her shriveled-up heart began affecting her body, as well. She lost the ability to see color and taste food. When attendants determined that she needed wounds to match Kaguya's, she no longer resisted and thus didn't need to be tied down.

Stimuli hardly even registered to her.

By the time whispers started floating around about Kaguya's ascension being imminent, Mayoi had become precisely what Yamato wished her to be. If they had told her to die, she would have thrust a blade into her belly without a moment's hesitation. The girl had been reduced to an unfeeling doll, waiting for the day she'd be expended.

But then she had a visitor.

"Heya there, Princess. 'Tis an honor but to be in your presence. That's what the kids say, right?"

*　　*　　*

A visitor by the name of Jade von Saint-Germain.

"…Who are you?"

It was the dead of night, and some person she'd never seen before had come knocking on her bedroom door. The *hyuma* man had a delicate physique. One look at him was enough to tell that he wasn't from Yamato, and he *definitely* wasn't with the Special Forces.

So then, who was he?

Mayoi cocked her head as she posed her question, but aside from that, her expression remained emotionless as she sat atop her futon.

By contrast, the man offered a reverent bow and an irreverent smile, although his shoulders slumped in visible dejection at Mayoi's response. "Yeesh, I get *zero* reaction for that? I get the vibe that you aren't really one for exclamation marks, but I thought you'd be at least a *little* surprised. I totally just bombed that, didn't I? That's an egg on the ol' face…"

He scratched his cheek, then asked if he could come in.

She had no particular reason to refuse him. Most people in her position would have been embarrassed or scared, but she hadn't felt those sorts of basic emotions in a long time.

"Be my guest," Mayoi said.

The man thanked her, then slid the door shut and introduced himself. "Guess I'd better start by dropping my deets, huh? The name's Jade von Saint-Germain, and as of today, I'm a new diplomat stationed at the Freyjagard embassy. 'Sup?"

That was enough for Mayoi to comprehend who he was.

However…

"Deets? 'Sup?"

…the unfamiliar words caused some confusion.

What were "deets," and how did one drop them? What was a "sup"? Mayoi hadn't the faintest idea.

An awkward look crossed Jade's face…

"I, uh, I was kinda hoping you'd pick that stuff up on gut feeling, but…'deets' is short for 'details,' and 'sup' is just 'what's' and 'up' mashed together. That's all there is to it."

"Ahhh."

…but after he explained himself, Mayoi finally understood his words. She'd never heard those expressions before. The world was a vast place, however. Satisfied with his explanation, she crawled out of her blankets, sat up straight, and bowed down on all fours. "I am Mayoi, second daughter of Yamato's Emperor Gekkou. It is a pleasure and an honor to meet you. In my ignorance, I failed to understand your greeting, and I would like to express my sincerest apologies for my rudeness."

"O-oh geez, so formal… Honestly, it was my bad for not speaking more clearly."

Jade gave the girl another few quick bows of his own. He looked perplexed, as though unsure what to make of this odd young woman.

At that point, Mayoi gave voice to a very reasonable question. "…Mr. Diplomat, might I ask what you're doing at my residence?"

Jade quickly changed gears and gave her another bright grin. "Well, I was introducing myself to Emperor Gekkou, Lady Hinowa, and Lady Kaguya earlier, but you weren't in the castle. I figured it'd be rude not to say hi to the whole imperial family. It's like when you move to a new neighborhood, you know? You gotta do things like this on day one. But if I'm being honest, I have another reason, too…"

"And what is that?"

"See, Lady Kaguya totally has it going on, so I figured that her sister must be a knockout as well. As a dude, I wouldn't have been able to live with myself if I didn't meet you and exchange contact info."

"A knockout????"

"Ah, sorry, my bad. Again. It means someone who's *super* cute."

"I see…"

Mayoi still struggled to comprehend some of Jade's vocabulary.

"But man, I was totally right. Heck, I was probably *underselling* you. You're, like, the spitting image of your sister. I practically had to do a double take."

"That's the way I was raised."

"Oh yeah? Well, hey, beautiful sisters, I can always get behind that!"

"Thank you for your kind words."

"Personally, though, you're more my type. Lady Kaguya's got her whole menacing aura thing going on, but you've got this frail vibe that makes a guy want to protect you. Like, a chivalry kind of deal. That sort of stuff always gets me right in the feels. I'm from the land of knights, after all."

"I see," Mayoi replied rather perfunctorily to Jade's compliments.

Although listening to an extent, she wasn't paying the conversation much attention, and the half-heartedness of her responses made that fact abundantly clear. Mayoi's emotions had weakened such that nothing roused her.

Even so, Jade didn't so much as frown…

"I don't know about you, but I want us to learn more about each other. Is it cool if I drop by from time to time? Real talk, there is *nothing* to do at the embassy."

…and he assertively closed the distance between them.

Why is this man so interested in a mere tool such as I, I wonder?

Jade's actions earned him a tilt of the head from Mayoi. However, her sole purpose was to die, so she decided this wasn't really worth fretting over. Choosing who she met and spoke with wasn't Mayoi's right, so she gave him an answer befitting her station. "I'm afraid that isn't up to me to decide..."

"Oh yeah? Well, then consider this me signing off on your behalf. Boom, it's a done deal."

"What?"

"Lookin' forward to getting to know you, girl."

Somehow or other, a decision had been reached.

Not even Mayoi could remain emotionless in the face of something like that. A hint of surprise crept across her expression. Ultimately, it was all still inconsequential. It didn't matter what was going through that strange man's head, nor did it matter if someone from her house found out she'd met with him. A tool didn't need to consider those matters.

"I look forward to getting to know you as well."

Mayoi took Jade's proffered hand and squeezed it.

All she was doing was following his lead with no expression or emotion...

"_____"

...yet she realized something by doing so.

Now that she thought about it, this was the first time in all her life she'd ever held another's hand.

From then on, Jade began visiting her roughly once a week.

"Mayoi, you gotta hear this. The other day, I went to this... What're those tea party things called again?"

"A tea ceremony?"

"Yeah, yeah, that. So I was with this important Yamato vassal guy at this tea ceremony, and they brought out some grub."

"They served you grubs?"

"Nah, it just means food. Sorry about the slang. Anyway, they brought out some food, right? But for the utensils, they gave me these 'chopsticks.' And, like, what the hell?! Using those things is crazy hard! I didn't even know how to hold them at first, and even once I got that down, my food kept slipping right out!"

"I see…"

"We were eating these simmered potatoes, and I kid you not, I dropped them on the floor right in front of this vassal guy's face. He practically laughed me right out of the room. How rude is that? And also, what's so fun about sitting around drinking tea with a bunch of dudes? Like, doesn't that defeat the whole point?"

"Tea ceremonies are a popular pastime among Yamato gentlemen."

"That's what they tell me, yeah. The point is, would you mind teaching me how to use chopsticks so I don't blow it so bad next time?"

"If you asked, I'm sure they would be more than happy to provide you with a knife and fork…"

"I mean, sure, but it's like…even though you guys have been ramping down the whole national isolation stuff under Emperor Gekkou's reign, chopsticks and tea ceremonies are still part of Yamato culture. It's my job to respect stuff like that. Plus, I can't stand it when I screw up the little stuff. Nothing pisses me off like having someone think I'm an idiot. That's why I gotta get my chopstick technique down before my next tea ceremony. C'mon, Mayoi, I'm begging you here!"

"…Very well. I suppose there's no harm in it."

"Thanks a million!"

The topics of their conversations ranged from Jade griping about his work…

"Hey Mayo-Mayo, I brought you something real cool today."

"You did?"

"Big time. Grandmaster Neuro wanted to see me, so I had to pop back over to Freyjagard real quick, and while I was there, I spotted something real nifty in the Drachen market. I was all, 'Mayoi's *gotta* check this out,' so I bought it."

"I see..."

"Ta-daa! A 'lemon' fresh from the Lakan Archipelago!"

"A...lemon?"

"Oh-ho? Judging from your reaction, this is your first time peeping at one of these bad boys."

"It is."

"Hee-hee-hee. I'm telling you, this is one tasty treat. I'm so glad I decided to shell out that dough. ♪ Go on, try a bite. I already cut this one up, so go ahead and take a big ol' chomp."

"Munch... (>x<)"

"Pfffft! Man, you should see your face right now!"

"~~~~~~~... Are these poisonous?"

"Nah, 'course not. They're just super sour."

"I think my cheeks are stuck like this."

"Yeah, it's pretty rough if you try to eat 'em straight, but if you drown 'em in South Freyjagard sugar, they are *choice*. Here, have this one."

"Munch... (>x<)"

"Ah-ha-ha-ha!"

...to strange items Jade purchased...

"Hurrah!"

"What is that noise you're making?"

"It's something you just kinda say when you're amped up or trying

to liven the mood. Everything just feels more fun once you start shouting it. Go on, give it a shot. Hurrah!"

"Hur…rah."

"No, no, no, you gotta mean it. Oh, and pro tip, 'whoo-hoo' is
basically the same thing but cuter, so it's a great choice for the ladies.
Hurray!"

"Whoo-hoo…"

"Don't be shy, now!"

"Whoo-hoo."

"I wanna hear an exclamation mark at the end!"

"Whoo-hoo!"

"Hurrah!"

…to bizarre cross-cultural exchanges. There was no real rhyme or
reason to the content of their chats. However, they always took place in
the dead of night, and they were always in Mayoi's bedroom.

After the first few instances, Mayoi realized what was going on. It
was obvious that Jade ensured the Special Forces members guarding the
Mayoi's residence were unaware of the clandestine meetings. She gathered that he'd even hired a ninja to help him get in and out of the building.
The structure wasn't especially well protected, but that the ninja was able
to enter so easily with Jade in tow meant they were quite skilled. Perhaps
they were even Special Forces deserters.

Mayoi didn't report any of what she discovered to the staff. She
told herself that, as a tool, it didn't matter who dealt with her or how.
And at first, she even meant it. Over time, though, that became an
excuse.

She started going to bed later and later each night, and began
thinking about Jade frequently. With every thought, something in her
chest stirred, although she couldn't decipher what it was.

* * *

Then, a few months after they started meeting...

"Whew, we finally made it. I gotta say, we ended up cutting it pretty close."

"*Pant... Pant...*"

Jade had taken Mayoi, and the two of them followed a fugitive ninja named Sasuke out late at night to climb a nearby mountain. They typically only spoke in Mayoi's bedroom, yet this time, Jade had insisted he had to show her something.

However...

"...It's pitch-black."

...Mayoi couldn't figure out what that could be for the life of her.

She had gone along with his requests as she always did, but... when they finally made it to the summit, there was nothing to see except the vast, bleak night.

Mayoi turned to Jade and cast him a bored look...

"All right, all right, hold your horses. I told you, it'll all make sense in a sec."

...and the man grinned back at her.

What was going to make sense?

She was about to ask as much aloud, but she never got a chance.

Light erupted—blinding and white and shining from one side.

Mayoi snapped her eyes shut by reflex, then slowly opened them so that they could adjust.

"Ah..."

Dawn stripped away the veil of darkness, replacing it with the *vibrant, colorful hues* of a pale-pink flower field that went as far as the eye could see.

"Is the view here unreal, or what? There are lotus flowers everywhere, and from this high up, you can watch the whole hill slowly turn pink as the sun rises. With how much of a shut-in you are, I figured you might not even know you had such a primo spot right by your house."

The sight before her left Mayoi speechless. As Jade gave his little speech, he reached down and plucked two of the lotus flowers growing by his feet.

"Here, take a whiff of this."

"*Snnfff. …!*"

"It's wild how sweet they smell, right? Back when I was a kid, I used to snack on these."

A nostalgic smile spread across Jade's face as he started to take Mayoi by the hand. There were a couple of other nice spots with good views, and he wanted to show her all of them.

Then he noticed something.

"Wait, hey, Mayoi, why are you crying?"

"B-because…*hic*… Because I…!"

The girl's voice was practically a scream, and she crumpled to the ground where she stood.

Her vision grew bleary from the tears forced out by swelling emotions, and she all but scooped at her face as she wiped them away. They were obstructing her view, and she resented them for that so much she couldn't bear it.

She never knew.

She never knew that sunlight could feel so warm.

She never knew.

She never knew that soil could smell so sweet.

She never knew.

She never knew that the wind could whistle so gently.

She never knew.

©Sacraneco

She never knew that the sky was so high up.

She never knew.

She never knew that the world was so full of color.

She never knew...

"I'm having...so much fun right now..."

...that being alive could be so much fun.

At long last, Mayoi understood the mysterious feeling in her chest. Spending time with Jade was returning what she'd lost.

Her world had color and flavor again.

This magnificent place was where she *lived*, and she was starting to care about it again.

All the emotions Mayoi had lost years ago were returning in force, and when she recognized this, tears came with no way to stop them. Mayoi sat on the ground, paralyzed by the weight of her feelings...and felt Jade take her hand.

"Hey, you know what we say when we're trying to turn a frown upside down?"

He hoisted Mayoi back to her feet...

"Hurrah!"

...and shouted.

It was the phrase he taught her weeks ago. The one that she never quite comprehended.

At the same time, though, it always managed to cheer her up.

"Whoo-hoo!"

Mayoi shouted as well. She needed to release everything bubbling up inside her, and although she remained ignorant of the word's meaning, she spoke it as loud as she could. And through her tears, a smile blossomed.

Three days later, Kaguya's coronation was set, and with it, the day Mayoi would kill herself.

It had been several years since Mayoi last saw Kaguya, but her sister came to hand down the order in person. For generations, Yamato had diligently carried out the sacrificial rite. The system made one small sacrifice to secure national peace, and now the time had come for another to be offered up for the good of the state.

Mayoi was their tool, and this was the task assigned to her. That was the imperial family's code, and up until recently, it would have been no exaggeration to say that dying was the sole reason for her existence.

Now that she'd regained her will as a living individual, however, she couldn't possibly fulfill her duty.

She wanted to see more of the sky.

She wanted to feel more of the wind.

She wanted to smell more of the earth.

She wanted to go more places—and she wanted to do so with *him*.

To that end, Mayoi prostrated herself before her sister with her forehead pressed to the tatami mat floor and begged for clemency.

She promised to leave Yamato. She swore to harbor no interest in usurping the throne. In return, she pleaded only for her life.

But her entreaty fell on deaf ears.

The imperial family's tool was broken, and she could no longer execute the customary performance. However, this upset fell within expectations, and there was a backup plan for just such an eventuality.

If convincing the tool to commit suicide was no longer an option, they would instead pin a fictitious crime on her and have the new emperor personally execute her for it, and pursuant to Yamato law, they would use an incredibly painful form of capital punishment referred to as death by sawing. Judging their own flesh and blood like that would serve to demonstrate the Yamato ruler's virtuousness.

As soon as her sister expressed resistance to the idea of killing herself, Kaguya sentenced her to death and incarcerated her in Azuchi Castle. Thanks to the Special Forces' covert work, Mayoi looked unquestionably guilty.

In her jail cell, Mayoi pushed her voice to its limits screaming for help. She wore out her throat, then tore at it, yet even as blood dribbled from her mouth, she shrieked with all her might that she didn't want to die.

None came to her aid.

Finally, Mayoi realized the harsh truth—she had no inherent worth as a person.

The pain and the sorrow were too much for her, and she collapsed into sobs.

"Pleeaase..."

Why her? Why was all of this happening to her? Being born slightly after Kaguya was the only thing she'd ever done wrong. So why?

"Don't make me...stop being me..."

That was all she asked.

It was her deepest wish to be granted permission to live.

A new guard entered and relieved Shishi, and although Mayoi was barely able to choke out words anymore, she made the same impassioned plea to him, too.

The guard didn't so much as stir.

As a matter of fact, he remained motionless...

...even as his head rolled from his shoulders.

*   *   *

"Eek!"

"Hey there, Mayoi. You okay?"

"J-Jade… But why?!"

As Mayoi froze at the shocking turn of events, a man called out to her—the very one she'd thought of so often in her cell. She spoke his name in surprise, but he quickly silenced her.

"Shhh, keep it down. There are more guards outside." The decapitated watchman remained perfectly upright, and Jade rummaged through the corpse's pockets as he explained. "Listen, when word arrived at the embassy that you'd killed some maids and were gonna get executed, I got *mad* spooked. I knew you'd never do anything like that, and I kinda freaked out a bit. But it was obviously a frame job, so I sneaked in here to bail you out. Real talk, I would've come sooner, but that punk-ass Sasuke was shaking in his boots."

"Shishi was here a moment ago. I can hold my own against any other, but that man is beyond my ability."

Mayoi searched for the latest voice and discovered that Jade wasn't alone outside her cell. The middle-aged ninja named Sasuke, who always helped him sneak into Mayoi's residence, was there, too. Sasuke wound his hands around each other and spooled back the thread he'd used to silently behead the guard.

"Sheesh, dude. Considering what I pay you, I figure you could at least *try*. I swear, you've gotta be the most useless fugitive ninja around… Ah, found it."

While griping about his ninja accomplice, Jade finally located the item he was looking for: the key to Mayoi's cell.

"There we go. Now we're all peachy—"

"Y-you can't!" Jade began to unlock the door, but Mayoi stopped him. "You'll get in big trouble!"

If Jade went through with this, he'd share Mayoi's fate. The prospect of him dying was so horrible that merely imagining it left Mayoi feeling like she would lose her mind.

The warning did nothing to give Jade pause, though…

"You've got a heart of gold. For real."

…and he unlocked the cell.

"Oh no…"

"But see, that's why out of all the people in Yamato, I wanted to at least save *you*."

"At least…?"

There was something peculiar about Jade's remark.

Mayoi was still sitting on the floor, so Jade lowered himself to her eye level to answer her question.

"I need you to listen close. Pretty soon, Freyjagard and Yamato are going to war."

His expression was normally so chipper, it bordered on insincere, yet there was no doubting the severity of this statement.

"What…? A-a war…?"

"I heard it straight from Grandmaster Neuro. The Four Grandmasters have been pushing Emperor Lindworm to conquer the rest of the continent for a while, and now that he's finished getting the nation under his thumb, he's formally decided to adopt their plan. And that means attacking Yamato. The army's already mobilized, and it's ready to begin the invasion at the drop of a hat."

"It can't be…"

"…To be honest, they wanted to storm the border *today*, but I went to Grandmaster Neuro and got him to hold off. I told him I needed enough time to rescue you."

"Huh…?!"

To rescue *her*? Mayoi couldn't begin to make sense of it. Jade was on the Freyjagard Empire's side. What did he care about someone in Yamato?

"Why...would you go so far...?"

"What do you mean, 'why'?! It's 'cause you're the most important babe in my whole life!"

"_____"

Jade grabbed Mayoi's shoulders and spoke with more passion in his voice than he ever had before. This time, Mayoi was at a complete loss for words.

Not long ago, back when she was just a tool, she might not have understood the significance behind Jade's statement. Now, though, his meaning came across loud and clear. She felt the same way, after all.

Mayoi was surprised, flustered, and thrilled... Feelings whirled inside her, intermixing and throwing the girl off-balance.

Jade rubbed his neck. "Here's the problem, though... Grandmaster Neuro didn't exactly agree to sit on his hands for free. The empire's got this scheme it's cooking, and the GM said that if you want Freyjagard's protection...then you have to help out with the plan."

"What...do you mean?"

"You know that grody-ass belfry, right by the inner castle?"

Mayoi nodded.

She came to Azuchi Castle infrequently enough that she didn't recall every detail, but the moss-encrusted belfry was distinctive enough to leave a mental impression.

"According to Grandmaster Neuro, that belfry is actually a secret magical artifact, and if you load it up with magic, it can amplify that spell and spread it across all of Yamato. He wants you to cast a spell that'll put all the Yamato soldiers to sleep."

"A-a spell?!"

Mayoi was surprised to hear about the bell's true function, but what shocked Mayoi most of all was the empire's plan. That her using the artifact was a condition for securing her clemency meant that it had to be possible, but there was a problem.

"But I…I don't know how to use magic…"

She had never so much as studied the subject, much less actually cast a spell. There was no way for her to meet Freyjagard's demand.

However…

"Don't you worry. Grandmaster Neuro gave me something nifty to help out on that front."

Jade's expression was downright dauntless as he retrieved an object from his pocket—a large black crystal that nearly filled his whole palm.

"This thing's an artifact called a Philosopher's Stone, and when you stick it in someone, it makes them 'evolve' by forcibly drawing out their potential… You might be wondering why Azuchi Castle has the bell if they never use it. Well, back in the day, they actually did. Grandmaster Neuro told me that long ago, the Yamato imperial family had this Administrative Authority magic they used to control all the native spirits in the nation. The magic's gotten weaker over time, and nowadays, it's totally shriveled, but that doesn't mean it's gone for good. If we use this Philosopher's Stone to draw out the power sleeping within you, you'll be able to use magic just fine!"

"I will…?"

Was it really that simple? Mayoi lacked the knowledge to answer that question with any certainty. The situation was shifting rapidly, and she had no time to consider her choice.

It was all so abrupt that Mayoi felt her head spinning.

And yet…

"The thing is, not even Sasuke has the skills to get both of us out of the castle. This plan is the only way to save us both. I'm beggin' you here, Mayoi… Please, come with me. I want to be with you. Now, and for the rest of time."

…Mayoi could see herself reflected in his eyes. He was looking straight at her.

She didn't understand what was going on, and it was impossible to know the right decision. However, if it meant a chance to be together with Jade, the man who was willing to let her live within his gaze, then Mayoi had no reason to refuse his proposal.

The plan Neuro entrusted to Jade went off without a hitch. Part of Mayoi's job was to act as a spare for Kaguya, so all it took was a change of her clothes, and the castle guards—few of whom had ever had any meaningful interactions with her—were none the wiser as to her true identity. She didn't even need to rely on Sasuke's disguise techniques.

By combining the bell's power with the ability to communicate with spirits the Philosopher's Stone awakened in her, Mayoi successfully instructed the spirits all across Yamato to go to sleep. The tolling of the bell also served as the signal for Lindworm's army to storm the Yamato border, and with the Yamato forces unable to fight, the Freyjagard soldiers annihilated them. Yamato lost a full third of its army in the span of a single night, and though their warriors' strength bought back some ground, the losses proved too much to overcome. The Freyjagard Empire overran Yamato with sheer numbers, and eventually, the nation lay in ruins.

Mayoi watched her homeland fall from the safety of the imperial army's protection with no regrets. And why should she have any? After all…

"You people…took everything from me!"

The castle tower was engulfed in flames. Angry cries thundered like an earthquake, but Mayoi was unshakable, and she met the shouts with equal fury.

Why should she have to die for the likes of them?

How dare they criticize her for not doing so?

It didn't make a lick of sense.

I'm not an idiot, you know…

Mayoi knew that Jade was an agent who'd been explicitly dispatched to win her to Freyjagard's side. His story had been fishy from day one. After all, what sort of respectable diplomat went and visited a sequestered princess's bedchambers just because he didn't get a chance to introduce himself? It was part of his plan.

Jade had heard about the imperial family's code and the way Mayoi was treated. His goal was to rise in station by playing a key role in the war effort against Yamato. To that end, he'd shown Mayoi kindness to make her into a puppet that would dance on his strings. Jade's compassion was calculated, and every sweet nothing had been a lie. None of it meant a thing to him.

Mayoi knew as much long before she betrayed her country.

But so what?

Jade's words were hollow and his kindness false, but his hand was the first she'd ever been offered. His kind words were the first she'd known.

Those lies showed Mayoi the fun of living.

She didn't care if it was all a lie.

She didn't care that he didn't love her.

She was fine with him using her.

Living solely for Jade's ambition was enough to sustain her heart.

It was sufficient.

Yet now…

"~~~~~~~~~~~~~~~~~!!!!"

Tears of frustration streamed from Mayoi's eyes, and she kicked the floor even as the flames scorched it black.

Ultimately, she'd failed in being useful to Jade.

Her life for him was unsuccessful.

That knowledge was so heartbreaking she couldn't help but sob.

Mayoi harbored little hope that Jade would forgive her.

He was going to hate her.

He would never look her way again.

He would never think of her.

He wouldn't even *remember* her.

Once again…she would be alone.

The world was vast, yet Mayoi was going to leave it by herself.

When she realized that, it hurt so much that her chest felt likely to rip apart.

She was abandoned, tormented by agonizing pain.

After finally meeting someone willing to see her as an individual, Mayoi knew the joy of living within his gaze, and she wanted to die in it as well.

"Darling… I miss…you…"

"What's that? You called?"

"………………What?"

Someone answered her.

Her plea that should have been lost amid the fire and chorus chanting for her death had reached a man who shouldn't have been there.

Mayoi nervously raised her head. It couldn't be. There was no way.

She looked out into the raging sea of fire. He was there, just beyond it. Standing at the room's burning entrance was Jade von Saint-Germain.

"Heya there, Princess. 'Tis an honor but to be in your presence. That's what the kids say, right?"

He wore the same irreverent smile he had worn during their very first encounter.

"D-dar...ling... But why...?"

"Whaddaya mean, 'why'? Whoa, c'mon, you can't be serious, right? What the hell kinda guy doesn't drop everything and come running when his girlfriend's in a jam, huh? I'm from the land of knights, for crying out loud!"

Mayoi was struck speechless. She'd believed his visage would never grace her eyes again, yet against all odds, they were reunited.

Jade, for his part, strode forward with his asymmetric grin...

"Whoops...!"

"Darling!"

...and tripped, tumbling to the ground by Mayoi's side.

When Mayoi got closer, she noticed something.

"Ahh! Y-your leg...!"

Jade's right leg was burned raw. Most of it was little more than charcoal now, and it was obvious at a glance that it was well beyond saving.

"Yeah, I tried to come through the hidden tunnel all gallant and badass, but, like... Apparently, shit's on fire? We're talking some reeeeeal nasty stuff. I got roasted on my way up here."

With a big grunt, Jade crawled his way to a seated position across from Mayoi. From this distance, she spied that his shoulders were heaving and his forehead was slick with sweat. Burns dotted his entire body. Jade must have climbed like a man possessed to endure the flames.

"Listen, Mayo-Mayo. I wanted to save you, but it looks like this is as far as I'm gonna get."

"Wh-why?! Why would you come here?!" Mayoi shrieked. What purpose was there in Jade willingly endangering himself as he had?

Jade flashed her his usual smile. "How many times are you gonna make me say it? It's about chival—"

"LIAR!!!!"

Mayoi wasn't going to excuse his obvious deceit this time.

"You're lying! I know it, and so do you! You don't love me one bit, *and I've been aware of that this whole time!*"

"Wh—?"

"So why come for me?! You're going to die!" Mayoi screamed.

How could he make such a stupid decision? Truthfully, Mayoi didn't care about Jade's reason. He was going to die, and that unacceptable reality drove her into a frenzy.

Upon seeing her reaction…

Wait, seriously? She found out?

…Jade was secretly shocked.

Not once had he considered that Mayoi knew.

Mayoi had accused Jade of not loving her, and she was correct. Jade didn't care for her one bit. On the contrary, he loathed the girl. She reminded him of his old self—his life in that mansion.

Back when I was weak, when all I could do was suck up to the people around me and go along with whatever they said…

Jade was a child of the Saint-Germain family, a lineage of renowned aristocrats. The name alone carried prestige.

However, that was only on Jade's father's side. His mother was a commoner and a prostitute. Although he was the offspring of the family head, Edgar, Jade was also the son of a whore.

Imperial nobles had a tendency to be selfish, but Edgar was a comparatively reasonable sort, and he took responsibility for Jade's mother's pregnancy by keeping her on as a mistress and moving her and Jade into his mansion. However, Jade's mother had an affair with one of the servants, then absconded and abandoned her child.

Being the son of a runaway mistress, Jade suffered terrible mistreatment. It would have reflected too poorly on the Saint-Germain household to kick him out altogether, but the abuse he endured was horrific.

Surviving that hellish crucible taught Jade his inherent lack of worth as a person.

That was what drove him to seek fame and status so desperately. He wanted to become valuable, such that none would harm him again.

Reading people had always been a talent of his. It started out as a way to protect himself, but in time, he developed it and formed connections to rise in the world. His ascent was meteoric, especially for the Freyjagard Empire, and after he enticed Mayoi into aiding the invasion of Yamato, he was named Yamato Dominion Administrator, a title on par with a dominion lord's.

Without him, the empire had no way of holding Yamato.

Jade had assumed that meant he'd changed. The worthless wretch was gone at last. No more would he cower and suck up to those around him, agreeing to whatever they said.

Mayoi's weakness reminded him of his own, though, stirring something in him every time he saw her.

And yet...

...he'd returned to her all the same.

Jade had scraped and clawed through searing flame to save her.

No...that wasn't it.

The effort was only another attempt to show off. A lie to conceal the pitiful truth.

I was running away...

After losing to the Resistance and forfeiting everything he'd worked so hard to build, Jade had nothing but his own worthless existence puffed up with fiction.

It was more than he could bear. Thus, he'd fled to the woman who would never turn on him.

God, I'm such a piece of shit...

Jade was sick of himself.

He never changed, and he'd failed to become a person of renown.

Were that true...

"Wait, you think I don't like you? C'mon, Mayo-Mayo. That's crazy talk."

...then he wanted to at least see his final deceit through to its conclusion.

In all the world, there was one woman who desired the man Jade genuinely was, and as a liar, this was the closest he could come to doing right by her.

"C'mon, what're you getting all neurotic on me for? Aside from the JK Game, I've never tricked you in my whole life. Plus, you think I really woulda come anywhere near this gnarly disaster if it weren't to save the lady I love?"

Jade wrapped Mayoi in an embrace. The hug was a falsehood, the kind he'd fed her countless times before.

And yet...

Huh?

...Jade could feel his arms tighten around her slender frame.

He was squeezing Mayoi so tightly that it was probably hurting her.

Not once had he ever held her this roughly.

Jade hurriedly tried to loosen his grip and discovered he was unable.

And as he sat boggling at his own actions...

"You're such a liar...!"

...Mayoi returned his embrace.

She folded her arms around him, dug in her nails, and *hugged him dearly.*

"I don't care if it's fake. I want you to stay with me to the end! Don't leave me all on my own!"

"_____"

The heat of their bodies against each other felt hotter than the fire, and between that, Mayoi's scream, and the intensity with which she needed him, Jade realized something.

He'd been laboring to build his worth for so long, pursuing it with single-minded devotion to the exclusion of all else.

Yet now that his life was on the verge of ending, he had someone he could hold with all his might, and who would hold him with all of theirs. Surely, there was value in that.

No noble. No lord. No emperor. Nothing.

Jade's feelings for Mayoi were so strong that he couldn't control his strength, and she felt the same. And if that was the case...

I've been worth something this whole time...

It may have only been in a single person's eyes, but to Mayoi, Jade was more precious than anything else in the world.

If only Jade had realized it before the point of no return. He'd always prided himself on being sensitive to matters of the heart, but when it came to his own, he was as dense as they came.

He had given Mayoi nothing but lies, and he'd hurt her repeatedly, but if she was willing to forgive him for all that, then starting now, they could share something new—the first *true* love in all Jade's life.

There were only seconds left, but they were plenty.

To Jade, every moment they spent holding each other was so joyful—so *fun*—that it was worth more than the rest of his existence.

"Hey, you know what I'd like? To see the lotus flowers again, just me and you."

"…Yeah…that sounds nice…!"

And with that, Azuchi Castle's tower came tumbling down.

❦ On to the Final Journey ❦

The Resistance uprising in the Yamato self-governing dominion ended with the dominion government's collapse, and although the inner castle tower continued burning for another few days afterward, it eventually died out. Now there was nothing but a mountain of scorched rubble lying where the palace had once stood.

Tsukasa wandered around the area.

If he listened carefully, he could make out joyful laughter coming from all directions. The people of Yamato were cleaning up the debris; theirs were the voices he heard. Kaguya hadn't needed to say so much as a word; everyone had gathered of their own accord. There were men and women, children and adults, and samurai and tradespeople all working together to get the job done under Kira's watchful supervision.

At the rate they were going, the castle would stand at its former glory in no time.

Mayoi's body had yet to be identified. There were many corpses among the wreckage, but all of them had been mangled so severely in the collapse that it was impossible to tell who they might have been. Still, there was no way she could have escaped the blaze, leaving little doubt that she was indeed dead.

Kaguya had made an announcement to that effect, and that was the way the people of Yamato saw it as well. Their rage at the traitor princess who manipulated them had been fierce enough to ignite the sky, but her death went a long way toward quelling that fury, and now every face in sight was marked with a sunny grin.

Tsukasa didn't hear a single person wax nostalgic about the prosperity they'd enjoyed under Mayoi's reign. He didn't know what it felt like to be mentally dominated, but he imagined that becoming Mayoi's obedient puppets caused tremendous pain and humiliation.

Those were the emotions that colored the past three years of their lives, and none of them would ever get that time back. There were so many things they'd lost and would never reclaim. Grief did little to slow their efforts, however. Citizens worked hard to prepare for the coming trouble.

The Freyjagard Empire had lost its self-governing dominion, and it wasn't going to be long before it came to take it back. Much as Kaguya and the people wanted to rebuild their nation, the empire wasn't going to sit back and let them.

The word on the street was that Freyjagard was currently locked in a fierce civil war between the Bluebloods and the official army led by the Blue Grandmaster. The battle was all but decided, though, and the few remaining Bluebloods were being hunted down and picked off. Once the empire had its house in order, it would inevitably take action against Yamato.

For Yamato to know lasting freedom, it would have to endure more conflict. The nation was weary, and the trial ahead was unimaginably grueling. If the people of Yamato were dismayed or anxious, they certainly didn't show it. They had been given a second chance at protecting their homeland, and their morale couldn't have been higher.

Tsukasa gazed at them, impressed. They were a strong people.

And Kaguya, the one uniting the citizenry, had already started preparing for combat with Freyjagard. The civil war restricted the empire's options, and Kaguya took full advantage of that opportunity to organize Yamato as swiftly as she could. She'd sent letters to her chief vassals and their heirs across the nation, calling for a meeting on the restoration effort.

During the interim, while her subordinates traveled to the capital, Kaguya invited Tsukasa for tea.

After satisfying Tsukasa's stomach with a light traditional meal, Kaguya served him some *koicha* tea that she'd kneaded herself. Meanwhile, Shura acted as her host's attendant and carried away meal trays so she could bring some teacakes.

Tsukasa knew the proper guest etiquette for Japan's tea ceremonies, and he responded to Kaguya's hospitality accordingly.

"I see you are well accustomed to traditional manners, angel," Kaguya noted with delight once Tsukasa had finished drinking his tea. "Hath our little hobby spread to the empire during these past three years, then?"

"No, the world I'm from coincidentally has a similar custom."

"Oh-ho. I must say, then, I fear your world places too great an emphasis on ceremony. Never before have I had a guest deliberately avoid drinking from the cup's front."

"Hmm. I think there's a certain beauty in following the fixed format and observing the nuances of the process." As Kaguya tittered and hid her mouth behind her sleeve, Tsukasa gave her a smile before lifting his empty cup again. "...And I must say, this really is a beautiful piece. The pale loquat hue is nice, and the way the texture of the ceramic glaze calls to mind the idea of permanence is simply stunning. But what impresses me most of all is how gently the clay sits in my hand."

In Earth terms, it was roughly akin to a *korai chawan* Korean tea bowl. In Japan, such relics would normally be kept in museum cases beyond anyone's touch, so holding one was exciting.

"Many of my vassals prefer to keep such precious items tucked away safely in storehouses, but I find that too great a waste to bear," Kaguya replied. "Vessels are not meant merely to be seen, but to be held and enjoyed as well."

"I imagine the cup itself is happier this way, too," Tsukasa agreed.

"I am told that the Lakan's 'white porcelain' cups of stone are gaining favor in the empire, but I find I much prefer clay. The whims of fire and chance ensure that each individual item has a natural texture different from any other, and the stoutness of the earth comes through each time a cup meets one's lips. No porcelain can offer that, I daresay. Still, I will confess to having an appreciation for the manner in which porcelain's makers seek out beauty in precision and for how they have hewn as much harshness from the taste of their craftwork as they possibly can."

"Porcelain's form and smooth surface cause the light to drape around it just so. It's the kind of uncompromising beauty that only humanity can forge. In every world and every era, the inquisitive way people fixate on beauty always surfaces in the humblest of objects. Things we drink from, things we serve food in—like porcelain, and this cup," Tsukasa said in admiration as he handed the cup back to Kaguya.

"All are moved by elegance, and all seek it out. Simply living is not enough to fill our hearts. The way we yearn for beauty is the very thing that makes us human," Kaguya replied. She tucked the cup away behind her back.

After clearing away everything that sat between her and her guest, Kaguya sat up straight…

"I thank you for accepting my invitation today. Once my vassals and their heirs arrive, I shall become quite busy indeed, so I had hoped to take this moment to return the favor for the meal you treated me to in the dungeon. Furthermore, I wish to apologize for the unkindness my people showed you and your cohorts in the time before I returned to the castle."

…and gave Tsukasa a deep bow.

"You have my deepest apologies. Nothing can excuse the way we leveled our blades at you after you accepted my brazen request and risked your lives to help us reclaim our nation. If it doth please you, we wish to take responsibility by presenting you with the head of our next Samurai General in compensation. At present, that is the greatest atonement we can offer you."

"_____"

Shura was next in line to become Samurai General, and when Kaguya offered up her head as part of her apology, she didn't so much as flinch. With eyes closed, Shura silently waited for Tsukasa's response. She had doubtless been prepared to pay for the misconduct with her life the moment she and the other samurai drew steel against the Elm delegation in the inner castle. If Tsukasa accepted, she would obey Kaguya's order without hesitation.

That willingness to lay down her life for others, and the culture that encouraged it, were both things unique to Yamato. The nation's isolationist policies had sequestered them from the rest of the world for a long time, and over that span, it had developed a rather unique set of values. And it was due to those principles that Tsukasa felt he needed to clarify something.

"We fought well and hard for this peace. I would just as soon not have any more blood be shed," he stated.

"I thank you for your lenience, angel."

"If we're talking compensation, though, I do have a few questions I'd like answered."

"Oh? And whatever might those be?" Kaguya inquired, raising her head.

Tsukasa directed his attention to Shura, who stood beside her ruler. "...I'm sorry to impose, but would you mind granting me and Princess Kaguya the room for a—?"

"Ah," Kaguya cut in. "'Tis about *that* matter, then. There is no need to pay Shura any special mind. As I mentioned, she is to be our next Samurai General. Knowing of Yamato in its entirety is a burden that her position demands."

Evidently, Kaguya had already deduced what Tsukasa intended to ask her about. He couldn't help but admire the young woman's insight.

"In that case...," Tsukasa began. "When Azuchi Castle tower got set on fire, Shura told me that Princess Mayoi had been slated for execution on charges of murder before she committed any treason at all."

"Indeed she was."

"And I take it...those accusations were false?"

"What?!"

The shocked yelp came from Shura.

Tsukasa ignored her and went on. "The first time I met Princess Mayoi, I sensed that her hatred for Yamato ran deep. She could have butchered its people and not lost a wink of sleep over it. Recognizing that was precisely what made me question the story of her crime. Hers wasn't the sort of loathing that could be sated by murdering a mere three maids."

"........."

"It wasn't until Aoi told me what she learned from Shishi, about the Yamato custom that's been going on for generations, that all the pieces fell into place. I had the sequencing backward. She didn't commit those murders because she was full of hate. She was full of hate because she was framed.

"I assume, then, that Princess Mayoi refused to take part in the ritual suicide. Thus, you decided to have her killed. You wanted to use her as a tool to convince the masses of the Yamato imperial lineage's nobility and virtue. In other words, the fault for Princess Mayoi's betrayal and the entire tragedy that followed lies with you... Or rather, with your lineage and its institutions, doesn't it?"

Shura's eyebrows shot up in rage. "How dare you! The princess would never—"

However...

"Indeed."

"...Huh?"

...the moment Kaguya confirmed Tsukasa's theory, Shura's anger turned to confusion.

"Prin...cess...? What...are you...?"

"Impressive as always, angel. I am awed at your piercing insight. To be seen through so thoroughly doth take from me my desire to mislead you."

As Shura stared in blank shock, Kaguya revealed the truth to the new Samurai General.

"For the three centuries in our recorded history, the Yamato imperial family hath always had a code. When one of us takes the throne, all their siblings kill themselves. Watching the royals comply with the harsh rule and lay down their lives inspires loyalty and pride in the people. That act forms the bedrock of Yamato's unity. However, there are aspects of the custom kept from the public. The brothers and sisters of the ruler do not surrender themselves of their own will for the sake of Yamato. Rather, they are raised for the sole purpose of dying when they are told."

"......?!"

"Aside from the firstborn, any child of the emperor's is immediately isolated in a residence on the city's outskirts and reared as a sacrificial lamb under the watchful eyes of the Special Forces. They are granted no freedom, nor permitted the joys of living, such that when the appointed day comes, they shall be a convenient tool so sick of existing that they shall embrace death without hesitation. Such was the way my sister Mayoi was brought up. However..."

Kaguya's face contorted in annoyance.

"...when the time came to pull her out of the storehouse for use, that fool refused to kill herself. Her death would have embodied the imperial family's devotion and fostered respect in the citizenry. Yet she had the nerve to abdicate her responsibility out of a petty desire to live... It should go without saying that I could not suffer that to stand, and the Special Forces and I were forced to employ our backup plan, branding that idiot a criminal and dispensing the death penalty."

"S-so wait, Princess, you...? You really...?"

The color drained from Shura's face, and Kaguya nodded.

"Indeed I did. Mayoi slew nary a soul, and for that matter, nary a soul was slain at all. She was innocent as a babe. The entire affair was a scheme concocted by the Special Forces and me. The angel accused me of inciting Mayoi to treachery, and I cannot deny the charge. However, the empire's invasion would have occurred regardless of my sister's actions, so I would ask that he not hold me accountable for that."

Kaguya sat with regal dignity even as she confessed this barbarous deed. In no way was she debasing herself. In her eyes, her actions carried the weight of absolute justice behind them.

"I... I... ~~~~~~~~~~~~~~!!!!" Shura could not agree. Her ruler's methods were too much to bear.

The wolf *byuma* hadn't so much as blinked when Kaguya ordered her to present Tsukasa with her own head, but now she looked downright horrified. Shura fled the tearoom as fast as she was able.

"...Are you certain that was the right call?"

Tsukasa had anticipated Shura's response. That was the whole reason he'd asked her to leave the room.

If Kaguya was concerned, she didn't show it. "I told you, did I not?

In time, Shura will become Yamato's Samurai General. She will need to know the whole truth, as her father Shishi did before her... Had you not asked your question, I would have told her myself in time. So please, your concern is unnecessary. Shura is a strong and intelligent girl."

Shura understood her position and knew that Yamato needed her strength in the coming days. Kaguya was confident that she would make her peace and elect to fight for Yamato with everything she had.

After expressing her faith in Shura...

"And? What shall you do now that you know Yamato's secret?"

...Kaguya trained her gaze on Tsukasa without sparing a glance for where Shura had fled.

"Will you inform the masses who serve me in ignorant bliss? Depending on how one looks at it, the imperial family's system could be judged akin to Mayoi's mind control."

"I certainly wasn't planning on it," Tsukasa replied, shaking his head. "In my opinion, there's a big difference between the way Mayoi forcibly distorted people's perceptions to serve her own ends and the simple act of selecting what information to release for the good of the public."

"Even if it doth mean sacrificing a helpless maiden?"

"I certainly don't feel good about your methods. Were I a *Yamato citizen*, I might be driven to action, but I'm not. I'm just a guy who'll be leaving this world before too long. As one who doesn't even live here, it would be ridiculous of me to upset any system that's created a three-hundred-year-long era of peace and enjoys massive popular support merely to appease my personal feelings."

The way Tsukasa saw it, this sort of issue was best dealt with by the people it affected. He and the others had aided the People's Revolution in Elm and the Resistance's fight in Yamato, but they'd only gotten involved because people had asked them for help.

Tsukasa wouldn't have done a thing otherwise.

This was no different from his abandoning Lyrule on the night the People's Revolution began.

A slight look of surprise crossed Kaguya's face at Tsukasa's answer. "Oh-ho. And here I was all but certain you would rebuke me."

If that wasn't his plan, though, then why had he pried so deeply into Yamato's secrets?

Tsukasa gave that unspoken query an answer. "You mentioned sacrificing a helpless maiden, but…Princess Mayoi isn't the only victim in your current setup."

"How so?"

"Generations of your emperors forfeited their children to that fate, and when you have kids of your own someday, they will be subject to it as well. The way I see it, Princess Kaguya, your duty is no less cruel than Princess Mayoi's."

"_____"

"*That's* what I wanted to ask you about. If you, a member of the imperial family who will be forced to sacrifice your own children, consider that a burden and wish to reform the system…then I'm willing to do everything I can to help you."

Tsukasa and Kaguya had been through enough together that they were more than strangers. If Kaguya felt trapped by her age-old customs and was struggling to escape them, Tsukasa was willing to help her to her feet. But only if she, as a victim, asked him to.

Kaguya's eyes had been still throughout the conversation, but when Tsukasa made his offer, they wavered like pools upset by tossed pebbles. The hesitation only lasted an instant, though.

The ripples quickly subsided, and Kaguya responded in her same dignified tone. "I appreciate the sentiment, but the sentiment alone shall suffice. I am Yamato's rightful heir, and unlike that fool who needed to do *naught but die*, my resolve is firm. The greatest good for the least cost. My father and mother shared that ideal, and the imperial family hath long held true to it. Flawed though it may be, it hath brought us the miracle of three hundred years of sustained peace, and I find that beautiful, as I do the Yamato that enjoys the fruits of that sacrifice. And this recent strife hath only tempered my feelings. There are those in this country who can survive nowhere but here, those who yearn deeply to live within these borders. It was the will of Yamato imperial families past that built us a history so beloved, and I intend to protect it until such a day comes when *the people of Yamato themselves* tear it down."

Kaguya was fine with devoting her life solely to that end. There was no doubt in her expression as she gave her answer. Pushing any further would be an imposition.

"Fair enough." Tsukasa nodded and stood. "Then I have nothing more to say. Thank you for clearing up my questions."

The Elm delegation's business in Yamato was concluded. The rest was up to the nation's people to deal with for themselves.

Tsukasa turned and headed to leave the room, and Kaguya called out to him from behind. "I should think that you, of all people, would understand. For, like us, you try to bring about the greatest amount of good for the least cost."

Her voice no longer carried the dignified, unshakable resolve that it had a moment prior. Now it was tinged with something akin to sorrow.

"So, as thanks for your concern, I shall give you a warning. The act of serving the masses in the hope of achieving the greatest good possible will end with you making sacrifices of yourself and those you care about. Humans can barely bring happiness to one, let alone a country. The more you try to save, the more shall slip through your fingers. This holds true for all, save inconceivable superhuman prodigies who bestow joy to all without the need for deception or pretense.

"So bear this in mind. If, knowing that you are but a common man, you would still try to aid as many as you can, know, too, that not a soul shall be able to accompany you on the harsh path you tread. Should you keep walking it, then in time, those you call friends and those you may court will cease to understand you, just as I lost Shura…and Mayoi."

"_____"

Tsukasa departed the tearoom and shut the door behind him.

"………"

The stifled sob Tsukasa heard through the door lingered in his ears for a long while.

"You still wish to cling to equality? To suffer in pursuit of that absurd ideal? All while knowing what people are truly capable of?! Surely you suspect there must be another way! You must know that the more you try to save, the more it all slips through your fingers…?!"

"Rgh…"

Both her sob and her warning called to mind the curse Gustav had left Tsukasa with before his death.

Tsukasa already knew that he was merely a man. Only a true prodigy could save everyone without forfeiting anything, and he understood that wasn't him.

Still, he'd sought more…

"You killed your own father for 'the people'? For complete strangers? You're insane!"

…and broken so many things in the process. Things that could never be repaired.

Tsukasa didn't need Kaguya's warning. He'd understood all along. No one else would truly understand him. It was a long-accepted truth. However, the reality was…no such flawless prodigy existed. Nobody could have saved more people than he did. They wouldn't have even tried. Thus, Tsukasa had no regrets. He regularly wondered if there were better choices he could have made, yet he never looked back and bemoaned his decisions. And he never intended to.

But if—*if*—it turned out there was someone like Kaguya described, who could make everyone happy in the truest sense of the word without needing to set any price or needing to resort to deception...

Would I be able to regret it then, I wonder?

"...Hmm?"

As Tsukasa walked through the remains of the inner castle, lost in thought, an object caught his attention, sparkling in the corner of his eye. At the bottom of the rubble heap, something small and shiny glinted like a needle in the soot and grit.

Tsukasa wondered what it could be, and he stooped down and swept away the detritus piled atop it.

When he uncovered the item...

Is this what I think it is?

...he gasped a little.

Then, not a moment later...

"Oh hey, we were looking for you!"

...he heard a voice calling from behind.

Shinobu and Ringo were hurrying over.

"Ringo's got something she wants to tell you!" Shinobu said.

"Just now...I was...looking back through...the satellite data. And there's...something...I noticed."

They must have been running around the perimeter of the castle's remnants searching for him, as Ringo's speech was more faltering than usual on account of her labored breathing.

Tsukasa...

"Sharing your findings won't be necessary."

...dismissed the girl's worry, however.

"Whatever you saw on that satellite feed doesn't change the fact that the battle between the Seven Luminaries and the Yamato self-governing dominion is over. Our work here is done."

"Oh..."

"Tsukes, are you...crying?" Shinobu asked.

"I got a little soot in my eye, that's all."

Tsukasa awkwardly deflected the question and reached into his pocket to retrieve a handkerchief. With it, he scooped up the pure-white sword shard from the ground, wrapped it up, and tucked it safely in his breast pocket.

This was no time to get hung up on questions that didn't have answers.

All the people of this world had things they wanted to protect, and Tsukasa and his fellow Prodigies were no different.

The philosophical quandaries could wait...until they were home.

And if they hoped to make that trip...

"Shinobu, I want you to pass this along to the others. At dawn tomorrow, we're leaving Azuchi and heading for the hidden elf village. Our strange journey across this world has taken us far and wide...but this next stop should be our last."

...it was time to get a move on.

Their destination was all but in sight.

AFTERWORD

Thank you all for buying and reading the seventh volume of *High School Prodigies*.

I'm Riku Misora, the author.

This time around, the *High School Prodigies* series finally got a drama CD! I wrote some short single-character pieces as Blu-ray bonus items back when the *Chivalry of a Failed Knight* anime aired, but this was my first time writing a drama CD script with a full-fledged story. I have to say, it was pretty tough.

Of course, the original plan was just to choose a scene from the books to be voiced, but then I jumped in and was all, "It's not every day these characters get to speak aloud, so I should celebrate by writing an all-new script!" so I really only have myself to blame, lol.

During the post-recording session, I couldn't stop myself from grinning like an idiot. All the characters sounded exactly as I'd pictured them, and I think all of you who bought the version of this book with the drama CD included will enjoy it, too!

A big thanks to everyone involved in its production!

Regarding the story, the latest arc was kind of an experiment for me. I like to think that it was able to capture a different sort of energy than anything else I've written to date.

Thematically, I wanted to try writing a love story between a scumbag guy and a scumbag girl, and I think I did a pretty all-right job. By the way, if you take a look at Mayoi in the illustration of the lotus field scene, you can see that her appearance changed pretty radically between the past and the present. The transformation came about because she wanted to forget her life as Kaguya's spare, so she bleached her hair and tanned her skin. Which look do you all prefer on her? Personally, I'm on Team Present!

This book marked the end of the Yamato arc. Starting next time around, the Prodigies will finally begin uncovering the truth about why they were called to this other world and what triggered their strange journey.

I hope you'll continue accompanying them for a little longer.

Here at the end, I'd like to take a moment to thank all the people who helped make this book a reality.

Sacraneco, thank you for the illustrations, which were as fantastic as ever! Especially those ones! You know, those ones! The pinup illustrations at the beginning! It's unreal how good they were. Unreal, I say!! I'll treasure them forever!!

I'd also like to thank Kotaro Yamada, whose art in the *High School Prodigies* manga adaptation never fails to astound. Oh, to get pinned down by Dr. Keine and made into a very good boy...

Furthermore, a huge thank-you to the GA Bunko editorial

department. We had to follow a pretty tight schedule this time, so thanks for sticking with me all the way through.

Finally, the biggest thank-you of all goes out to all you readers who've supported this series. I hope you enjoy the rest of the *High School Prodigies* story, and let's meet again in the eighth volume.

HAVE YOU BEEN TURNED ON TO LIGHT NOVELS YET?

86—EIGHTY-SIX, VOL. 1–11

In truth, there is no such thing as a bloodless war. Beyond the fortified walls protecting the eighty-five Republic Sectors lies the "nonexistent" Eighty-Sixth Sector. The young men and women of this forsaken land are branded the Eighty-Six and, stripped of their humanity, pilot "unmanned" weapons into battle...

Manga adaptation available now!

WOLF & PARCHMENT, VOL. 1–6

The young man Col dreams of one day joining the holy clergy and departs on a journey from the bathhouse, Spice and Wolf. Winfiel Kingdom's prince has invited him to help correct the sins of the Church. But as his travels begin, Col discovers in his luggage a young girl with a wolf's ears and tail named Myuri, who stowed away for the ride!

Manga adaptation available now!

SOLO LEVELING, VOL. 1–6

E-rank hunter Jinwoo Sung has no money, no talent, and no prospects to speak of—and apparently, no luck, either! When he enters a hidden double dungeon one fateful day, he's abandoned by his party and left to die at the hands of some of the most horrific monsters he's ever encountered.

Comic adaptation available now!